“You Are No More Ready To Walk Away From Me Than I Am From You,” Geoff Said.

“And if you want to lie and pretend that you are, you’re welcome to try. But your body is telling me a different story.”

“You’re right,” she said in a low husky voice.

“Then we’re agreed.”

“Agreed?”

“That th[illegible] your bed.”

“Geoff, I’[illegible] idea.”

He kissed h[illegible]t ask permission or do it tentatively at all.

When he lifted his head, she was breathing heavily and her hands were on his shoulders, and she tried to draw him back to her. She stared up at him with lust in her eyes and underlying vulnerability that made him wonder if this was a mistake. But then he remembered he was Geoff Devonshire and he never made mistakes.

Amelia Munroe was going to be his, and now they both knew it.

Dear Reader,

I'm both excited and sad that this is the last of THE DEVONSHIRE HEIRS books. Geoff is the oldest of the heirs and bound mostly by duty and familial responsibility. His heroine is Amelia Munroe—she's a tabloid darling, a millionaire heiress who's known mostly for her scandalous behavior.

Geoff and Amelia travel in the same circles most of their lives but have never had a chance to get to know each other until recently. So it's just Geoff's bad luck that a stipulation in his father's will is making seeing Amelia so difficult. She's always had a pack of paparazzi following her around and he is supposed to keep out of the papers.

But they are fiercely attracted to each other, and nothing is going to keep them apart.

I hope you've enjoyed meeting all of the heirs!

Happy reading,

Katherine

KATHERINE GARBERA

HIS ROYAL PRIZE

Silhouette® Desire
Published by Silhouette Books
America's Publisher of Contemporary Romance

Recycling programs for this product may not exist in your area.

ISBN-13: 978-0-373-73027-8

HIS ROYAL PRIZE

This edition published by arrangement with Harlequin Books S.A.

For questions and comments about the quality of this book please contact us at Customer_eCare@Harlequin.ca.

Visit Silhouette Books at www.eHarlequin.com

Printed in U.S.A.

Recent Books by Katherine Garbera

Silhouette Desire

†*His Wedding-Night Wager* #1708
†*Her High-Stakes Affair* #1714
†*Their Million-Dollar Night* #1720
The Once-A-Mistress Wife #1749
***Make-Believe Mistress* #1798
***Six-Month Mistress* #1802
***High-Society Mistress* #1808
**The Greek Tycoon's Secret Heir* #1845
**The Wealthy Frenchman's Proposition* #1851
**The Spanish Aristocrat's Woman* #1858
Baby Business #1888
§*The Moretti Heir* #1927
§*The Moretti Seduction* #1935
§*The Moretti Arrangement* #1943
Taming the Texas Tycoon #1952
‡*Master of Fortune* #1999
‡*Scandalizing the CEO* #2007
‡*His Royal Prize* #2014

†What Happens in Vegas…
**The Mistresses
*Sons of Privilege
§Moretti's Legacy
‡The Devonshire Heirs

KATHERINE GARBERA

is a strong believer in happily-ever-after. She's written more than thirty-five books and has been nominated for career achievement awards in series fantasy and series adventure from *RT Book Reviews.* Her books have appeared on the Waldenbooks/Borders bestseller list for series romance and on the *USA TODAY* extended bestseller list. Visit Katherine on the Web at www.katherinegarbera.com.

To all of the ladies on the Jaunty Quills blog
who let me know I wasn't alone when I felt like I was—
thank you.

Prologue

Geoff Devonshire didn't have time for the biological father he'd never met. He had a jam-packed schedule and little time for much else today. But his curiosity was piqued, so he'd decided to attend this meeting at the Everest Group's corporate headquarters. His own office building was two doors down in a very posh section of London along the Thames next to the controversial cucumber-shaped city hall.

When he got off the elevator on the executive level, he was escorted to the boardroom at the end of the hall.

"Hello, sir. You are the first to arrive for the meeting. May I get you something to drink?"

The pretty, efficient secretary directed him to a seat at the table and when he declined a drink, she left.

Geoff walked over to the glass-lined wall and looked down at the river Thames. It was midmorning in March, and the sun was peaking through the heavy clouds that hung over the city.

The door opened behind him and he turned as he heard the secretary greeting another person. It was Henry Devonshire—one of his half brothers. The former rugby captain was now known for his celebrity reality shows.

They had never met before, and knew nothing of each other except what was in the press.

"Geoff Devonshire," Geoff said, offering his hand to Henry.

"Henry," he said, holding out his hand.

Geoff felt a bit strange meeting this man for the first time in his life. But the door opened again before he could say anything more and Steven Devonshire walked in.

All three of Malcolm Devonshire's illegitimate sons were now in the same room. Geoff realized that gossip magazines and celebrity Web sites would pay a fortune for a photo of the gathering.

Edmond, Malcolm's solicitor and all-around errand boy, stepped in and invited them to have a seat. Geoff sat back and watched the other men. Malcolm had admitted to fathering the three of them but had never really been a part of his life except to send a check once a month.

His mother, Princess Louisa of Strathearn, despite her lofty-sounding title, was a minor member of the current royal family. She had been a party girl and had relished her affair with Malcolm and the tongues it caused to wag. Until she'd realized she was only one of three women Malcolm was wooing. She retreated to her country estate and to Geoff's knowledge had rarely left in the years immediately after his birth.

Henry's mother was '70s pop singer Tiffany Malone. Henry was the middle son.

Steven, the youngest son, had been born to Lynn Grandings, a Nobel Prize-winning physicist. There had been a bit of a brouhaha when it seemed that both Geoff and Steven would attend Eton, but Geoff's mother had sent him to an exclusive boarding school in the States instead in a well-publicized exchange with a prominent senator's son.

Scandalously, they were all born in the same year with just several months between their birthdays.

"Why are we here?" Henry asked.

"Malcolm has a message for you," Edmond said.

"Why now?" Geoff asked. It seemed odd to him that their father would finally assemble the three of them in a room.

"Mr. Devonshire is dying," Edmond said. "He wants the legacy he worked so hard to create to live on in each of you."

Geoff almost got up and left. He wanted nothing from Malcolm Devonshire. He never had. Malcolm had devastated his mother. And as a man with two sisters, Gemma and Caroline, Geoff couldn't abide any man who would treat a woman so callously.

Edmond passed three file folders across the table to each of them. Geoff took his time opening the folder. He wasn't sure what he expected to see inside, but the handwritten note was a bit of a surprise.

Malcolm wanted him to run the airline unit of the

Everest Group and if his unit out-performed the other two, he'd inherit the chairmanship of Everest Group.

Geoff quickly assessed what running a business unit of a busy corporation would mean. Though flying was his passion, he'd never aspired to owning a commercial airline and his own business interests kept him very busy. But he wasn't about to just walk away from this. This was his chance to take what Malcolm had worked so hard to build and...what? A part of him was tempted to ruin it. Run it into the ground. He didn't need the money and his mum wouldn't take a cent from Malcolm. She had her own money.

While Henry and Steven talked to Edmond, Geoff leaned back in his chair. Edmond turned to him.

"Your thoughts?" Edmond asked.

"I don't need his money," Geoff said. He'd also inherited a title and a fortune from his maternal grandparents. He had never had to work a day in his life but he'd always pursued business with passion. His interests were varied and diverse but he liked to keep busy.

"May we have a moment to discuss this alone?" Steven asked.

Edmond nodded and left the room. As soon as the door closed behind him, Steven stood up. Geoff noted the way Steven moved, very carefully with controlled measure. He'd heard a little about him and the china company that he'd brought back from the brink of bankruptcy. Steven was a man with a lot of business acumen. Geoff suspected he'd be very hard to beat in this competition that Malcolm had set out for them.

"I think we should do it," Steven said.

"I'm not so sure," Geoff replied. "He shouldn't put any stipulations in his will. If he wants to leave us something, so be it."

"But this affects our mums," Henry said.

Everything that Malcolm had done since Geoff's birth had affected his mum. And Geoff wasn't sure what the outcome would be. His mum, Louisa, didn't want anything to do with Malcolm. But Geoff wanted something on her behalf. Something from Malcolm to make up for what he'd taken from her.

"It does affect them," Geoff said, thinking it over. "I see your point. If you two are in then I'll do it as well. But I don't need his approval or his money."

The men agreed. In the end the consensus was that they would accept the challenge laid down by the father none of them had ever met. Geoff left the building with Henry, who was quiet on the way down.

"Have you ever met him?"

"Malcolm?" Geoff asked.

"Yes."

"No. You?" Geoff had always assumed that Malcolm wasn't involved in any of their lives. He'd be surprised if he found out differently.

Henry shook his head. "It's interesting, this proposition of his."

"Indeed," Geoff said. "I have no experience running an airline."

Henry laughed in a genial way. "Nor I a record label."

"I have a feeling Steven has a leg up on us," Geoff said. "Look at what he did with Raleighvale China. I am used to running charitable foundations and businesses with a healthy cash flow."

"Me, too. That's the understatement of the year," Henry said.

After they parted ways, Geoff sat in his car in the garage, thinking about how he was going to add Everest Air to his already busy life. He'd find a way. He always did when it came to his responsibilities and duties.

Just once, though, he'd like to find something that was just for him. He did his family duty by attending royal functions and events that were important to his mother or sisters. Now he was going to try to turn a company that was owned by the man who had sired him into a profitable enterprise.

He wasn't doing it out of duty. He was doing it because he wanted to take his father's company and exceed all expectations, making it into a very profitable business. More profitable than his father had ever dreamed.

Geoff liked the challenge that was before him. Henry and Steven were both worthy adversaries, and meeting them under these circumstances seemed fitting. This was his chance to prove to himself that, as the eldest Devonshire bastard, he should enjoy the lion's share of the inheritance.

One

The event that same evening was long and boring—the kind of charity dinner that he'd rather not attend. But he was a Devonshire and a member of the British royal family and there were times when he simply couldn't decline. At least the William Kent Room at the Ritz was an exquisite venue.

His date for this evening was Mary Werner, the daughter of a billionaire office supplies executive. She was a suitable girl and would make him a proper wife, if that's what he was after. He knew that her family probably expected a proposal soon.

His half sisters—Gemma and Caroline, who were twenty-three and twenty-one respectively—called her his maiden bride. He pretended to growl at them for it but he knew they were right. Mary, as lovely as she was, was a bit too tame for him.

There was a spate of camera shutters clicking at the entrance to the ballroom. He glanced over his shoulder to see Amelia Munroe smiling for the photographers. She wore a bright red sheath, which hugged her generous curves, and held a small dog in one arm. The animal yipped whenever a flash went off.

There was a lull in every conversation in the room as all heads turned toward her. She said something in her distinctively brash American accent and then threw her head back and laughed. Suddenly he didn't mind being here quite as much.

"Oh, it's Amelia," Mary said quietly.

"Indeed. She does like to make an entrance."

"Yes, she does. Everyone is watching her. I wonder how she does it," Mary mused.

Geoff knew exactly how she did it. She drew attention because of the way she was built, the way she smiled, the way she laughed. She moved like a woman with loads of confidence. Her curly black hair was pulled up on her head and tendrils fell around her heart-shaped face. He couldn't see her eyes from here, but he knew they were a diamond bright blue. Men wanted her—hell, he did. And if Mary's reaction was any indication, women wanted to *be* her.

The atmosphere in the ballroom had changed. Though the paparazzi were kept at the door, the excitement spilled into the room as Amelia walked in.

"I guess the International Children's Fund must be one of her pet charities this year," Mary said.

"Must be," Geoff said. Hubert Grace, one of his stepfather's friends excused himself from the table and

Geoff shook his head as Hubert made his way across the ballroom to Amelia's side.

"What is Hubert doing?" Mary asked.

"I have no idea. I suggest we go back to our conversation, though," Geoff said.

He might be attracted to Amelia but he knew from past experience that the things he wanted most in the world were the ones that were dangerous to him and to his peace of mind. And with this new deal he'd agreed to with Malcolm, he had to be on his best behavior—something that had never failed to make him restless.

"Good idea. I wonder if she realizes how much of a distraction she is," Mary said.

"Does she bother you?" he asked.

Mary shrugged. "Not really."

Mary was a beautiful girl—a proper English rose with fair skin and thick, straight hair. Her eyes were a pretty blue that showed her keen intelligence. But she was tame. She allowed herself to follow the rules…much like he did on occasion. Their position oftentimes meant that they had to do what society dictated, especially in their circles.

He glanced back over at Amelia holding court across the room. He wanted to be over there but not one of the crowd. Given his rank and status in society he rarely settled for being one of the many, and this time was no different.

"Not really?" he asked Mary. "What is it about her that you envy?"

Mary took a sip of her wine and then turned to look at Amelia, who was still engaged in conversation with Hubert. "Everyone is watching her and talking about her—even me. I guess…I just wish I could walk into a room and make everyone else want to be me."

Geoff studied the American woman. She was gorgeous, from her kissable mouth to her curvy body. But more than that, it was her joie de vivre that drew his eye. She'd grown up rich and often turned up in *Hello!* magazine and YouTube video on her yacht in the Mediterranean. She'd had her share of scandals, but she never shrank from the public eye. He was intrigued by her.

"I think it's the fact that she doesn't follow the rules and doesn't care if anyone is bothered by that," Geoff said.

"I agree," his sister Caroline chimed in as she returned to the table. "You are talking about Amelia, right?"

"Yes," Mary said. "I envy her."

Caroline laughed. "I'm jealous of the way she commands the attention of everyone. I wish I did."

"You do, Caro, you just don't realize it."

"I think you might be the only one who thinks that," she said, smiling up at him. He adored both his little sisters, having practically raised them. His mum had bad episodes of depression and often took to her room for weeks at a time. And his stepfather had died when the girls were four and six years old.

"The right man will see that as well," he said.

"And when will he come along?" Caro asked.

"When you are thirty," he said with a mock growl.

"Until then, I'll just have to have fun with Mr. Wrong."

"Not if I have anything to say about it."

"You don't," she said with a giggle. "You are too busy running Everest Air."

He scowled. Malcolm's "gift" was a pain in the ass. With the spike in crude oil prices and the slowing economy, the air industry was feeling the pinch. Geoff was coming up with some creative ideas to keep the airline in the black, but it was taking up more time than he wanted to devote to his job.

He decided it was time to start working hard *and* playing hard.

"Too true, Caro," he said.

Mary was quiet during their conversation and he suspected it was because she was expecting an offer of marriage from him soon. As much as he liked Mary, when he tried to imagine spending the rest of his life with her, he couldn't do it.

She was simply too quiet. He had more fun talking to his sisters then he did talking to her, and in the end he guessed that made the decision he'd been mulling over about marrying her so much easier. It wasn't fair to Mary or himself. They both deserved more from their relationships.

He had a life of duty and obligation, and he wanted his marriage to be more than a merging of family names and titles. He wanted the real thing—unlike what he'd seen in his parents' lives.

He knew that he could never turn his back on his responsibilities but he also knew that he'd always had in the back of his mind the fact that he was going to have a good marriage.

His mum's affair with Malcolm Devonshire had changed her. She'd said as much more than once when she was having her dark spells. And her marriage to Caro and Gemma's father had been made purely to restore the reputation she'd destroyed with her affair.

So he'd seen the obligation side of marriage and it had left him feeling empty. When he'd been younger, he'd seen his sunny mother wither whenever she read an article about Malcolm until she spent more time in her home then she did at the social obligations she used to enjoy.

And he knew he wanted more than that. He wanted someone different—a woman who could stir his passions. He heard the husky sound of feminine laughter and glanced across the room to where Amelia held court with several eager young suitors. He wanted her.

She spent a lot of time in the spotlight, something that he'd learned to avoid as a young man. But that didn't seem to bother him at the moment.

Geoff was used to going after what he wanted and used to getting it, and Amelia Munroe would be no different. He was going to have her.

He took a sip of his martini and leaned back in his seat as the emcee talked on and on. He thought back to the time he'd spent with Amelia on a philanthropic trip to Botswana. He remembered how compassionate and sincere she had seemed there. Not the spoiled heiress whose every move was catalogued by the press, but a woman who'd sat in the dirt and comforted a child who was crying. A woman who'd spoken the local language to the people who were collecting the water and medical supplies that their group had brought with them. She'd casually mentioned she'd learned the language on a trip years earlier to the same region.

Seeing that side of Amelia had intrigued him. But seeing her tonight in full form had reminded him that she was a complex, confusing, beautiful woman. One that he was suddenly hell-bent on getting to know better.

Amelia Munroe smiled at Cecelia, Lady Abercrombie, and nodded as the older woman talked about the fiasco at her dinner party a week earlier. Amelia wished she were indeed the careless person she was portrayed as in the tabloid media because then she could just walk away from Cecelia. But she couldn't. Lady Abercrombie was one of her mother's closest friends and when she wasn't rambling on endlessly, Amelia genuinely liked her.

"Well, to make a long story short," Cecelia said, "be glad you didn't come."

"I'm not glad I missed your party. It sounds like it was very interesting."

"If you'd been there, it would have been more than interesting," Cecelia said. "How was Milan?"

"Wonderful. Mother has designed a new line that is going to be simply spectacular. I can't wait for the world to see it."

"I'm going next week for a sneak peek," Cecelia said. Though in her early fifties, Cecelia looked at least fifteen years younger, with a trim, athletic build and perfectly coiffed blond hair. But what really made her look young was her smooth skin—something that Amelia's mother, Mia Domenici, attributed to the spa treatments Cecelia had twice a year in Switzerland. Something Amelia's father never approved of.

"I'm sure you'll have a lovely trip," Amelia said.

"I can't wait. Oh, I see Edmond, Malcolm Devonshire's man of affairs. I want to find out how Malcolm's health is, dear, do you mind?"

"Not at all," Amelia said and watched the other woman walk away. Cecelia was a gossip and always knew every detail of the personal lives of their set. She turned to survey the room and saw a man walking toward her.

She knew him in an instant. Geoff Devonshire. They attended many of the same functions and served on the board of the International Children's Fund together.

There was something about the man, with his dark, thick curly hair and piercing blue eyes, that she couldn't resist. She thought back to a photo she'd seen of him once, standing next to his Learjet in a pair of slim-fitting jeans—and no shirt.

Yummy. The man had chest muscles like the Italian models that her mother hired for her fall shows.

But unlike most men, Geoff had never paid her much attention. It was maddening, actually.

"Good evening, Geoff," she said, as he stopped in front of her. She stood up to give him the customary kiss on each cheek, but he startled her by putting his hands on her waist and brushing his lips against hers. Her mouth tingled from the contact and she tilted her head to the side to study him, trying to hide the fact that he'd caught her so off guard.

She was the outrageous one!

"That was a bit friendly," she said.

"I can be a cheeky bastard," he replied with a half smile.

"As can Hubert," she said.

Geoff laughed as she gave the older man a wave.

"Scandalous," he joked.

It was an apt choice of words, Amelia thought. Scandal might as well be her middle name. Though she had been born to a world of wealth and privilege, she'd also been born into scandal. Her mother had been the mistress of Augustus Munroe, a married New York hotel mogul who had changed the way that people traveled. He'd revolutionized the hotel industry with his signature luxury-themed hotels.

"But I don't want to talk about Hubert," Geoff said, staring her down with his impossibly blue eyes.

She took a sip of her champagne. "You don't? What *do* you want to discuss?"

"Dinner. Tomorrow night."

"Why, Captain Devonshire, are you asking or ordering me out?" she asked, using one of Geoff's many titles. She was playing coy but was surprised. After ignoring her for so long, why was he suddenly interested in her? He'd been a decorated war hero in the first Gulf war with the Royal Air Force.

Geoff smiled. "I'm asking, of course."

"But aren't you serious about Mary Werner?"

"We have been dating casually. Is that a problem?" he asked. "I didn't think that exclusivity was something you usually bothered with."

Heat rushed to her face. Geoff thought he knew her, based on what? Stories he'd seen splashed in the papers? She had always been careful not to repeat her mother's mistake of dating and falling for a committed man.

"Maybe you don't know as much as you think you do," she said.

"There's no maybe about it," he replied. "I'm sorry.

That was rude and I have no excuse for it. Please accept my apology."

"Accepted," she said. "You should know as well as anyone that just because a story is on a Web site or in the tabloids doesn't make it true."

"Give me a chance to make it up to you with dinner," he said.

"Why? Are you just after the girl you've read about?"

"No, I'm not," he replied. "There is something about the girl behind the headlines that intrigues me."

Amelia was afraid to believe him. Geoff was different from every other man she'd met but that didn't mean she could trust him. She had learned little about Geoff from the rumor mill—just that he was a man who took his work and his life very seriously, putting duty first. She had thought they had little in common—she courted the media and he shied away from it.

"If you have dinner with me, there will be photos and stories about us," she said, wanting to make sure that he understood what her life was all about.

"I am aware of that."

She nodded. "Then I will see you tomorrow night."

"I will see to the details," he said. "I'll pick you up."

"See you then," she said. She turned and walked away. She was always the first to walk away. She'd started doing that when she turned twenty-one and realized that she didn't have to wait for someone to leave her again. Someone...she meant her father and all men.

Geoff was different, though, and that made it all the more important for her to walk away. She needed the power to be in her hands and not in his. He had knocked her for a loop by brazenly asking her out while sitting a few tables away with his date. What did this mean? Did Geoff even know, or was the attraction between them that he'd denied so long simply too strong for either of them to contain?

She busied herself with the crowd of B-list celebrities she was hosting at her table in an effort to get her mind off Geoff. She knew that most of them had accepted her invitation to this event in hopes that they'd get a photo with her that would end up in tomorrow morning's papers.

She danced with each of the men at her table, trying not to notice where Geoff was. When it was time for her to go up to the front to narrate the slide show that documented her recent trip to Botswana, she found herself distracted by images of Geoff on the trip.

She remembered seeing him talking with the local businessmen, and helping out when a citizen had a flat tire. He seemed to be more than just a handsome face, more than a man who was doing his duty because it was expected of him. Though she'd been surprised that he'd asked her out. It would be nice to spend some time with a man who was more than he appeared to be.

Geoff started to return to his table but was stopped when he felt a hand on his arm. He glanced over his shoulder to see Edmond standing there. Geoff had been at numerous functions with Malcolm's right-hand man, yet this was the first time that he'd been approached by him in public.

"Yes?"

"I need a word."

"Certainly," Geoff said, leading the way through the crown to a quiet alcove. "What's up?"

"I saw you speaking to Amelia Munroe..."

"So?"

"I wanted to remind you of the stipulations of your father's—"

"Of Malcolm's will? He's never wanted anything to do with me, Edmond. I'm not going to let him dictate my life now."

"Understood, sir. But please be careful. I don't want you to lose your share of the Devonshire fortune."

Geoff walked away from the older man without responding. He was more than frustrated with the entire situation. He thought about just walking away, but his mother deserved something for the happiness that Malcolm had stolen from her.

Geoff returned to his table in time to greet Mary as she left the dance floor with Jerry Montgomery. Jerry was a nice enough fellow—an American sports reporter who covered British sports for ESPN. He had a toothpaste-ad, American smile—super-straight white teeth and a confident grin.

For some reason Geoff had never really liked the fellow. He couldn't say why and didn't spend a lot of time thinking on it. But Mary liked him. In fact she was flushed from dancing. She gave Jerry an intimate smile as he walked away. Geoff realized that Mary liked him. He also realized that he wasn't jealous in the slightest. In fact, he was relieved.

"Nice dance?"

"Yes. I simply love that song," she said. The song

in question was "I've Got You Under My Skin," made famous by Frank Sinatra. The song was a standard that evoked memories of his mum teaching him how to dance.

"I'm glad he offered his services, then."

"Me, too," she said somewhat shyly. "Where is Caroline?"

"Gone for the evening. She said this party was too tame."

"I guess it is, by her standards. By yours as well," she said. There was a question in her voice as her eyes cut across the room to Amelia.

"Ah, well, this is the kind of function that I have to attend."

She smiled then, the closest thing to a genuine expression of joy that he'd seen all evening. "Duty calls."

"Indeed it does. But I've had enough for tonight. Shall we?"

Geoff saw Mary home but didn't feel like heading back to his luxury townhome in the leafy-green area near Greenwich. He was restless and not sure what he needed, but he knew that sitting at home wasn't it.

Actually, he did know what he needed, but he couldn't have it until tomorrow night.

Normally, when he felt this way, he got in his plane—his favorite classic 1983 Lear—and took off for a few days. When he was in the sky he wasn't Geoff Devonshire, bastard son of Malcolm and Princess Louisa of Strathearn. Instead, he was simply Geoff and there were no rules, no obligations and no one who wanted anything from him.

Instead, he found himself at a club just off Leicester Square where a friend of his deejayed. He entered through the back to avoid the paparazzi who covered the red-velvet rope area and found a small booth in the rear of the darkened club.

The electronic beat of the music pulsed loudly and he felt everything inside him stir as his thoughts again turned to Amelia. He wanted to make sure she had no ill feelings regarding his comment about her tabloid life. He called his butler, Jasper, and asked him to send Amelia a little gift, something he thought she'd appreciate. And something that would show her that he saw her as more than just the scandal girl the world thought they knew. He'd picked up a carving in Africa he'd seen her admiring—maybe he'd known all along he was going to ask her out. He jotted a note on his personal stationery that he had Jasper bring him and sent the man on his way.

His mobile phone rang and he glanced at the caller ID before answering it. It was his vice president at Everest Air. Given the time of night, it probably wasn't good news.

"Devonshire here."

"It's Grant. We have a major problem. My contacts with the baggage handlers union said they are getting ready to strike."

"We don't employ them, the airport does. Right?" Geoff said.

Running the airline was taking some time to adjust to. As a former RAF pilot, he knew planes and understood what it took to fly them. And as a businessman he knew how to make money, but there were intricacies to the airline business that he was still learning.

"That is correct."

"So let's talk to their boss and see what we can do to sweeten the deal. Who is in charge?"

Geoff heard the rustle of papers on the other end of the line. "Max Preston."

"Let's have him to the office tomorrow. Pull out all the stops and make sure he knows that we want to listen to him. Listening is key in these situations."

A lot of his team at Everest Air was waiting for him to prove himself, to show them that he had the right stuff to run the company. And Geoff wouldn't have it any other way. He'd spent a lifetime making sure that everyone knew he didn't coast through on his father's coattails.

"I've had to deal with all kinds of hostile people, including rebels in Uganda who didn't think that my foundations had any business there. But I sat down with them, I listened and the rebel leader talked," Geoff said, remembering that long night when he'd sat across a fire from a man with an AK-47 cradled in his arms as he expressed the same desires that most men had. A desire to be heard and treated fairly. These were things that Geoff couldn't provide but he had been able to promise he would talk to his friends in government and was able to successfully gain some concessions for the rebels.

"I had no idea. I thought you just travelled around partying with your other rich friends."

"Grant, are you jealous?"

"Hell, yes, mate. Who wouldn't want that jet-set life?"

"It's not as glamorous as you might think."

"Nothing ever is. What time are you thinking for this meeting tomorrow?"

"Early. We want Max to have time to go and talk to his people once we've talked to him."

"Will do. I'll let you know when it's arranged," Grant said.

Geoff smiled to himself. "That's perfect. We want to make sure that no one's travel is disrupted because of this baggage handler situation. I think your suggestion is spot on."

Grant laughed. "Thank my wife for that one. She made the suggestion over tea."

Geoff smiled to himself. Women were able to sometimes get to the heart of an issue. Something he'd learned from his sisters and his mother.

Grant was going to be a great asset to him at the airline. He had been working there for the last three years, and though the profits weren't surging under his leadership, they had been steady.

Geoff knew from his own business interests that constant vigilance would be the key to making sure that every quarter increased their profit margin. And he could do that with men like Grant on his team.

Winning the competition against his half brothers was important to him because this was a family thing. And he always succeeded when he put his mind to it.

He looked at his watch and realized he'd spent exactly two minutes not thinking about Amelia. Her grin flashed in his mind and the scent of her perfume lingered with each breath he took.

He couldn't wait to see her tomorrow night and get

to know the woman behind the glare of the paparazzi flashbulbs because he was having a hard time reconciling the two very different sides of her that he'd seen. She was a puzzle that he wanted—needed—to solve.

Two

Amelia loved London in the morning, despite how crowded the city was with workers heading to their offices and tourists rushing from palaces to Big Ben. To be fair, her morning started after rush hour and well into the congestion charges that were in effect in her neighborhood. It was a crisp, spring morning. She put on a pair of running shorts, a sports bra and a pair of sneakers and headed out the door.

But her cell phone rang before she'd hit the elevator. She glanced at the caller ID to see that it was her older brother, Auggie. She shook her head and thought about letting it go to voice mail, except the one time she'd done that he'd been reaching out for help.

"Morning, Auggie," she said.

"Sis, I need a favor."

She leaned against the wall in her foyer. Why was she

surprised? Her brother was the kind of man who always needed something. But she had almost lost him to drug use, and she'd made him a promise that if he got clean, she'd always be here to help him stay that way.

"What kind of favor?"

"I can't make the Munroe Hotels board meeting this afternoon. In fact, I need the entire week off. Do you think you can cover for me?"

"No, Auggie, I can't," she said. Auggie had a serious problem with responsibility. Though she was the one who somehow always made it into the papers, Auggie truly lived his life as if he didn't owe anyone anything. His therapist had told her to stop enabling him.

He was only eleven months older than she was, and given the circumstances of their birth and highly dysfunctional family, they'd had only each other to rely on while they'd been growing up.

Her parents were passionate lovers who couldn't keep their hands off each other, but they didn't know how to relate to each other outside the bedroom. They were both a little too self-absorbed to be good parents. In essence, she and Auggie had raised themselves.

"Lia, please?"

This was the hard part, she thought, because despite everything she loved Auggie and didn't want to have to tell him no. "I really can't. I have to be at the Munroe Foundation this afternoon. I'm presenting my report on Botswana."

"Can't you just reschedule it?" he asked.

She rubbed the back of her neck. If she did this for him, he'd start expecting her to run both arms of her family business again. Amelia had chosen the foundation because she liked the work. And Auggie had taken the public role of running the Munroe Hotels chain. She'd had to do a lot of behind-the-scenes "helping," since it appeared that Auggie hadn't inherited their father's business savvy.

"I can't."

"Lia, I'm not going to be there. If you aren't going to stand in for me, the board will probably decide to hold an emergency election for a new chairman and then there won't be a Munroe at the helm."

Her father would be very angry if they both missed the meeting. Amelia didn't want to do anything that would invite her father back into their lives.

"This isn't fair. You know I'm not supposed to run both organizations. I can't do it, Auggie."

"It's your decision, Lia. I think it might be better to let someone else take over."

"Do you want to make Dad crazy?" she asked. Her brother had a love-hate relationship with their parents. And while she tried her best to keep the peace from a distance, Auggie did his best to make sure that their parents were always a little bit uncomfortable.

Auggie chuckled. "That wouldn't bother me in the least."

Her dad was recovering from open-heart surgery and Amelia didn't want to upset his progress. "I'll do it. But you have to be back in the office in one week's time. If not, then I'm going to ask to have you removed. I'm not going to keep covering for you."

"You're the best, sis. Talk to you soon," he said, hanging up.

She ran every morning in Hyde Park and this morning

she really needed it. Auggie was frustrating beyond belief, but he was her brother. She passed tourists who were following the Princess Diana Memorial Walk and heading up toward Buckingham Palace for the changing of the guard later in the morning. She ran, trying to forget everything and enjoy the city under her feet as music blasted in her ears.

She should be thinking of her day or of this weekend's luncheon with her father but instead she was thinking of Geoff Devonshire.

He had the kind of brooding good looks that put her in mind of Mr. Darcy in Jane Austen's *Pride and Prejudice.* Objectively she thought that it was interesting that a man with aristocratic breeding would still fit a mold that was over one hundred years old. But then she had to laugh. Men hadn't changed in all that time. Women had been subject to their whims then and still were now.

The psychiatrist her mother had sent her to when she'd turned thirteen had said that Amelia had father issues. And that was still true.

She was always trying to prove herself to some man and Geoff would probably be no different. As much as she wanted to think that she didn't care, a part of her did. A part of her wanted to be at that quiet banquet table he'd occupied last night rather than at the center of attention.

His respectable girlfriend and his sisters had surrounded him. He had been born into scandal, as she had, but instead of being consumed in the paparazzi storm, he'd found a way to make a respectable life for himself.

In some way, she craved what he had. But then she

shook the thought aside. She was the media's favorite subject because she always did something outrageous. The very things that had gotten her on the cover of the weekly magazines had also gotten her father's attention.

Father issues, indeed.

At the entrance to her building she noticed Tommy, the photographer who always seemed to be following her, lounging against the wall. He had worn jeans, a baggy T-shirt and a khaki vest with lots of pockets crammed with lenses and backup batteries.

He snapped to attention as he saw her approach and took several photos as she entered her building. She suspected they'd show up on some Web site before the day was done. She'd probably replace whichever celeb they'd caught doing something unglamorous.

"Good morning, Ms. Munroe. There is a package for you."

"Thank you, Felix," she said to the doorman, taking the FedEx package that he held out to her.

Felix also handed her one of her own monogrammed towels and a bottle of water. She smiled at the Brazilian doorman. Felix did a good job of getting tips from her by always saying yes to all her little requests. He was very handsome and he'd come to the UK to find fortune as an actor, but he had found that his grasp of languages wasn't as good as he'd thought, so he'd started working here to improve his English.

She took the elevator up to her penthouse and entered the room. Lady Godiva was waiting for her. The miniature Dachshund was always happy to see her.

Amelia took a moment to pet her before walking over

to the floor-to-ceiling glass windows that lined the east side of her apartment. She sipped her water as she looked out over the city.

She wiped the sweat from her face, tossed the towel on the floor and looked at the package. The return address was from London. Someone had sent her a package last night.

Geoff Devonshire.

Lady Godiva danced around her feet with a tennis ball in her mouth. Amelia reached down and scratched her under the chin. Then she took the ball from the dog, tossing it across the room.

The dog scampered off after it and Amelia sat down on the arm of her black leather sofa and opened the package, intrigued.

What would he send her?

She pulled out a box wrapped in white paper with Geoff's monogram on the center of it.

For a moment, she couldn't make herself open it. She didn't want to think of Geoff as a real option. She just wanted him to be a sexy guy she was going to have fun with.

Not a man who would make her care.

"Stop being silly," she said to herself. She tore the wrapping and opened the box.

Her breath caught as she stared down at the exquisite African carving. She knew he'd gotten it in Botswana—she'd seen the carving when they'd been touring a village. Had he noticed her admiring it?

A piece of fine linen stationary was lying on top of the carving with a simple note.

I look forward to learning more about the woman behind the headlines.

Amelia told herself that he was simply trying to woo her, but her heart beat faster anyway. His actions had touched her. She took the carving into her bedroom and set it on her chest of drawers where she could admire it from anywhere in the room.

Steven called him at eleven and asked if they could meet for drinks later that evening. He wanted all three of them to have a chance to talk. Geoff knew it would be tight—he planned to take Amelia up in his plane and get away from the city. He knew that she liked the spotlight, but Geoff had learned from his mother that living under constant scrutiny made life difficult at best, and he thought she'd like the escape.

"Sure, I can do that. Why don't we meet at one of my clubs?" Geoff suggested.

"Just tell me where and I'll text Henry," Steven said.

Geoff made a few notes and took down Steven's mobile number. He'd never thought about having brothers before and at thirty-eight he worried he was a little old to start forming close relationships with Henry and Steven, but he was willing to try.

"Can I ask you a personal question?"

"Go ahead," Geoff said.

"Do you ever wish you'd gone to Eton? So we could have met earlier in life?" Steven asked.

Geoff had never thought about that. Growing up with sisters in his mother and stepfather's family, he'd often wondered about his father and the two half brothers he'd never met. But he'd known that meeting them would have devastated his mother, who wanted nothing to do with any of "Malcolm's mistresses' children."

"Sometimes. But I think we needed to live our independent lives," Geoff said.

"That we did. I'm looking forward to speaking to you later," Steven said before ending the call.

That was abrupt, he thought as he leaned back in his chair and spun toward the window that looked out in the direction of Heathrow Airport. This view from Everest Air was different from his office in the heart of London. His life had always been in flux and he'd always embraced change—he wondered if it was because of the way he'd grown up.

Why was he suddenly being so philosophical? He suspected it had to do with Malcolm's presence in his life after all this time.

He booked a table at one of his clubs and figured out exactly how much time he'd need to leave to pick up Amelia.

She was on his mind the rest of the afternoon. Only when Caro arrived to chat with him about a garden party their mum was throwing at the end of the month was he able to think of something else.

"I need your help, Geoff."

"You always do," he said with a smile.

She stuck her tongue out at him. "Mum wants to make sure that we have privacy. She doesn't want the party to be swarming with media."

"That's not a problem, Caro. They have never come to Hampshire and they won't now, especially not for this party. Henry is the one who is keeping them captive and with his very public persona, it should stay that way. I don't want this to weigh on anyone's mind."

She nodded. "I'll let Mum know."

"You do that," he said.

She smiled at him. "How's your maiden bride?"

"She's not mine." After last night's flirtation with Amelia, Geoff had barely given Mary a single thought. The vehemence of his response to his sister's question surprised them both.

"Really? I thought you two were getting serious."

He shook his head, but he wasn't about to discuss his love life with Caro. "Who are you dating now?"

"Paul Jeffries."

"The footballer?" he asked. Footballers were notoriously full of themselves and changed girlfriends with the passing of a season.

"The same."

"I don't like that. He's too…wild for you."

"Too bad," she said with a cheeky grin. "I'm twenty-one now. You can't tell me who to date anymore."

Geoff looked at her sternly. "If I see one photo of you in the weekly rags, that's it."

She glanced at her watch. "Oh, look at the time. I've got to run."

"Caro?" She stopped at his office door. "I'm just trying to protect you."

"I know. Love you."

"Love you, too."

After she left, he wondered if perhaps he should be taking his own advice. Amelia embodied everything that he warned his sisters to stay away from. Not a day went by that he didn't hear some juicy tidbit about her on the *One Show.*

But he was different than Caro or Gemma, and he knew how to handle Amelia. Besides, he was a man used to getting what he wanted, and he wasn't about to let anything stand in his way.

She intrigued him. He'd first started noticing her on their last trip to Botswana. Something about seeing the woman who'd had a salacious video on YouTube sitting in the dirt with hungry, sick children had piqued his curiosity. She was complex, he'd realized, and he wanted to expose all the layers of the woman to get down to her core.

Dating her was going to be hard with his busy schedule and hers. He needed a solid reason for the two of them to spend time together.

He stood and stretched. Glancing out the window of his office he saw the Munroe Hotel chain logo in the distance and he had an idea. If he could partner with Munroe Hotels and create unique travel packages for the Everest Air consumer he would be able to positively affect the bottom line of the airline. It was precisely the kind of idea he'd been searching for. Something that would help him win the competition with his half brothers and give him a reason to spend more time with Amelia.

But did party-girl Amelia spend any time in the offices of Munroe Hotels? He'd have to research it and find out. He made a few notes on his legal pad. He and Amelia both came from similar backgrounds, with parents who were more interested in themselves than in their kids.

He'd always understood that the Everest Group was Malcolm's life, and besting Malcolm on his own turf appealed to Geoff. He liked the feeling that thought evoked. And he smiled to himself as she finished making plans for his evening.

He made reservations at a little African restaurant that he hoped would remind Amelia that they had met in Botswana. He wished he'd had the time to get to know her better then.

When they'd been on the charity trip to Africa neither of them had obligations that took up their time. He could have spent all of his time focused solely on her. But that didn't bother him. He was more than ready for Amelia. He only hoped she was ready for him. The real man, not the staid one that she might expect from his reputation.

Amelia wasn't used to waiting around for some man, so it unnerved her a bit that Geoff was coming to pick her up. She'd spent the afternoon at the foundation office presenting her findings and persuading the board of directors to adopt her proposal for the course of action they needed to take.

"Why are you nervous?" Bebe asked as the sat in a pub near Waterloo Station.

"I'm not," she lied. It was ridiculous to have nerves like this before a date. It was nothing more than a date. He was just a guy—one she would go out with once or twice. She'd dazzle him with her smile and her winning personality and then…he'd move on. The way men always did.

"You are such a liar."

"Bebe—"

"Don't 'Bebe' me. Anyone else might believe that you are perfectly confident, but I know you better and you are nervous."

Bebe was her best friend and had been since they'd met at finishing school. The two had bonded when they were both ugly ducklings. Bebe had been overweight with frizzy hair, and Amelia had had braces and been gangly. They'd been an odd-looking twosome back then. None of their classmates would have predicted that they'd turn out to be incredibly successful and renowned for their glamorous lives.

"He's different. I know he's not going out with me so he can get his photo in the society pages."

"So you don't know how to treat him?" Bebe asked.

"I'm not sure that's it," Amelia said. The after-work rush hour had just started and people were hurrying past the window on their way home.

"Whatever it is, be careful. You don't want to do something outrageous."

She swallowed hard. Bebe was right. She couldn't afford to let her nerves get the best of her—she tended to act without thought or restraint when that happened, and that meant regrets.

"I'll be fine. One more glass of wine and I'm set."

Bebe smiled at her. "You look fab. I love turquoise on you."

"Thank you, darling. My mother recommended it."

"How was Milan?"

"Fab," Amelia said, winking at her friend. "In fact, I brought you back a little something."

She handed Bebe the shopping bag that she'd carried in with her.

Bebe took the bag from her but didn't open it. "What's going on with you? You're not yourself. Is it more than that yummy Devonshire heir?"

Amelia shook her head. Bebe was the one person in the world who knew about all of Auggie's troubles, and a part of her wanted to just unload on her friend. But she knew exactly what Bebe would say. *Don't enable.*

Hadn't she heard those exact words from everyone before? She knew that she was to blame. She should just step out of the equation, but letting the Munroe Hotel chain go wasn't something she was ready to do yet.

"Nothing."

"Is it Auggie?"

Amelia shook her head in disbelief.

"How do you do that?"

"I know you. And it isn't that hard to figure out. You just visited your mum and everything's okay there. Your dad is recovering nicely from his surgery, so that leaves Auggie. What'd he do this time?"

"He needed some time off from work."

"And you covered for him?" Bebe asked.

"Please, don't. I know I shouldn't have, but I'm not ready to walk away from the hotel chain yet."

Bebe reached across the table and squeezed her hand. "I don't want to make you feel worse when things are already mucked up. Tell me everything."

Amelia spent the next thirty minutes talking to Bebe about the board's ultimatum that she take over running the hotel chain if Auggie was going to continue skipping out on meetings.

"Are you going to do it?"

"I have no idea. I could run both the foundation and the hotel chain, but that would mean giving up my life. I mean, I'd have to work 24/7 to make it happen."

"You can't do that," Bebe said.

Amelia knew that. Sometimes she wished she simply were the scandalous heiress that the tabloids made her out to be because it would be so easy to walk away from it all if she were that shallow.

She needed balance and wanted her life to be more than just her charities and her family business. She wanted to come home to more than Lady Godiva and to have someone who cared about her. Someone who would take care of her the way she watched over Auggie.

"I have until the next board meeting to decide. So that's three months."

"You'll come up with a plan," Bebe said. "I'm here for you, whatever you decide. Just be sure that you're doing what's best for you."

Bebe gave her a hug as they stood up to leave. As they walked out, Amelia heard whispers about her as she passed. She put on her carefree smile and walked through the crowd. She wasn't sure she could keep that smile in place all night but she was going to try her damnedest.

Bebe was the only friend who knew there was more to her than her party-girl image and she intended to keep it that way. No matter how much time and money she donated, the media never covered that. Instead, they only printed stories about who she was seen with. She was afraid to let anyone see the real her, afraid that she'd lose a part of herself if she did, and she wouldn't be able to handle that.

Geoff seemed to be different than the other men she'd dated before but she was afraid to believe in that. Men had let her down and she had a hard time trusting her judgment as a result. For all she knew, he could be just like the rest of them.

Tonight she needed to be poised and sure of herself. She didn't want him to guess that she'd spent extra time thinking about her outfit or what she would say. She wanted him to see the woman the world thought she was. A hotel heiress with nothing on her mind but the next big party.

That would be harder than it sounded, she thought. Being that vapid took a lot of work. She smiled at the bellman as she walked into her apartment building and went up to her apartment.

Her sweet little dog was waiting for her and she scooped her up and held her close. For a minute she wished she didn't always have to be on when she walked out her front door. And she almost wished that she could let her guard down and share with Geoff how difficult it was to keep up the illusion of Amelia Munroe.

Three

Amelia laughed and all heads in the restaurant turned to look at her. Geoff was getting used to the fact that she commanded attention—and took his breath away as well. She was charming and funny, something he'd already known from the time they'd spent together in Africa. But tonight, despite the impression he'd had, she didn't even seem aware of the attention she garnered. Her focus was entirely on him.

"So there you were, caught by your superior in a compromising situation. What'd you do?"

"I told him I was doing my duty for queen and country."

She laughed again, and it was then that he realized her laughter never reached her eyes. She was laughing because the story was meant to be funny but there was something upsetting her.

"Are you all right?" he asked.

"Yes. Why do you ask?"

"Your eyes."

"My eyes?"

"Yes, I can tell that you aren't really engaged in what I'm saying. Don't get me wrong—you're a wonderful audience. But your heart isn't in it."

Those very eyes of hers widened. "How did you know?"

"I just do. What's on your mind?"

"It's not worth discussing. Especially when I'm having dinner with a sexy guy like you."

Geoff reached across the table and captured her hand. He stroked his thumb over her knuckles. "I'm more than just a guy."

"Sexy guy," she said.

He was tempted to let her distract him from the topic, but he knew this was a chance for a real conversation and he wasn't going to pass it up.

"That's not going to work. Later on, when I claim my goodnight kiss, we can talk about how sexy you think I am. But right now I want to know what's on your mind."

She turned her hand over in his and threaded their fingers together for a moment before pulling her hand back. "It's a bit heavy for a first date."

"You and I are beyond first-date stories. Tell me, Amelia."

"I have to—" She shook her head. "I can't do it. I know you mean well, but if I tell you about this, then we certainly won't be having the date you signed up for this evening."

He knew there was a lot more to this woman than met the eye. Now he was going to find out just how much more.

"Trust me. I'm very good at keeping confidences."

"Are you?"

"Yes. And no matter what else happens between us, I'd like to believe we are at least friends."

As a flash of surprise flickered in her eyes, he realized that she wanted to believe that, too.

She leaned forward. "I…how much do you know about my family?"

"We have a bit in common in our births, don't we?"

"Yes. Well, you have more in common with my brother. My parents married before I was born."

"But there was scandal around you both."

"Yes, there was," she said, then shook her head. "You really don't want to hear this. And to be honest, I don't think I want to tell you. Please, let's go back to enjoying our evening. Tell me more stories from your RAF days."

Geoff leaned back in his chair and took a sip of his wine. Letting this go would be so easy to do. It might be the gentlemanly thing to do. But he was more interested in being real than anything else. He wanted to know the girl behind the image. He wanted to be more to Amelia than every other man she'd gone out with. He wanted to know the real woman, and just now, he'd had a glimpse of her and he couldn't go back.

"I do want to know," he said quietly. "My family is complicated as well. I know that it's not always easy to balance our own lives and still take care of familial duties."

"You've just made it sound as if we have more in common than just our scandalous births?"

"We have a lot in common, love. We already know that from the time we spent in Botswana."

"I guess we do."

She cut a piece of her filet mignon and took a delicate bite. He waited, hoping that if he gave her some space and showed her he could be patient, she'd let him in, even if just a little.

After a few moments she put her fork down and leaned in close again. "I'm not sure I *can* talk about it. I don't like to."

"Just tell me what's troubling you," he said. "You can trust me." He needed to know what was on her mind. It hadn't taken him very long to figure out that Amelia was everything he'd hoped she'd be and more. She was smart and sassy and so damn sexy that he'd had a hard time keeping his mind on the conversation. Until now. She was in pain—he could see it. And he wanted to be the one to help her.

"I have to find a way to convince the board of directors at Munroe Hotels to keep my brother in his position as chairman. And I have no idea how to do it without throwing myself into running the company full time."

He was surprised. He'd expected her answer to be something else. Anything else, really, except this.

"Do you know anything about running the chain?" he asked.

"Plenty. I've done it before. But with my responsibilities at the Munroe Foundation, it's too much work to do both."

"And your brother?"

"He's not...well, simply put, he's not a man like you, Geoff."

What kind of man did she think he was?

"In what way?" he asked.

"He has never put family and his responsibilities before himself, and I have the feeling he never will," she said. "The thing I have to decide is if I'm going to keep covering for him, or let him sink and let my father's dream of keeping the hotel in our family die."

Amelia knew she was saying too much. But there was something in Geoff's beautiful, stormy blue eyes, something in the way he held himself and the way he leaned in when she talked, that invited intimacy and made her want to tell him all her secrets.

And that was dangerous.

She didn't mind sharing about Auggie and the Munroe Hotel chain, but there were other secrets that she knew she'd have to be careful to protect. Secrets that would be very damaging to her if Geoff didn't prove to be the man she was starting to believe him to be.

She doubted he had any idea that she held an MBA from Harvard, since she'd gotten her degree under her mother's maiden name to keep the paparazzi from following her there. Or that he had any clue that she'd been the one to run the chain in the late nineties since Auggie was the figurehead then. She'd kept her name off everything while her brother was in and out of rehab. Those were the type of tidbits she'd been careful to keep out of the public domain. She'd found that if anyone saw beyond the party-girl image she'd carefully cultivated they were confused, and often expected things from her she simply couldn't give.

"Why are you trying to save your brother's skin?" he asked. "Isn't he older?"

This was a mark of the man that Geoff was, she thought. That he saw her as a little sister and therefore someone who should be cherished and protected. She knew that much from watching him interact with Caroline and Gemma. Everyone knew that although the women were his half sisters, Geoff would do anything for them.

"Auggie and I are almost twins—only eleven months apart—so I don't really think of him as my older brother."

"He should," Geoff said.

She smiled at him. "I guess the rumors about you are true."

He arched one eyebrow at her. "Which rumors?"

"The ones about you putting your family first," she said. As much as she knew that many people would say she had a better family situation, Geoff had the real family, something that her parents had never managed to create.

Amelia had realized early on that having parents who were married but couldn't stand each other was hardly an advantage. And her parents' public fights had often managed to feed the fire of tabloid gossip about them.

What would it have been like to grow up with someone looking out for her?

And would that really have been any better. Because if her childhood had been different she wouldn't be the woman she was today.

And as Sandra Bullock said…"I complete me." Those words could definitely be applied to her. And she needed to remember that.

"What are you thinking?" he asked.

"I'm sorry. Let's stop talking about this. I don't need you to solve my problems."

"I don't recall offering anything more than a shoulder."

"Touché."

"I have an idea that will be beneficial to both of us," he said.

"What?" she asked.

"A venture between Munroe Hotels and Everest Air. It will give you something to take to your board of directors and it will give me a new line of revenue at Everest Air."

"Why do you need a new line of revenue?" she asked. She'd heard rumors there was a competition between the Devonshire heirs, but the details had been kept close to the brothers. Would Geoff trust her enough to tell her what was going on?

"I need an edge to make sure that my business unit outperforms Steven's and Henry's. We're competing with each other—did you know that?"

"I did. I don't know the details… You could use the paparazzi to help your cause…."

"I can't. That's not my way, but what do you think about my offer?"

"I'll think about it," she said.

There was a commotion at the front of the restaurant and she turned to see Tommy and some of his paparazzi friends scuffling with the maitre d'.

"I hope you don't mind seeing yourself in the papers," she said.

He tipped his head to the side and studied her carefully. "Why do you think they follow you around the way they do?"

"Probably because I invited their attention. When I was younger I didn't realize how my actions were goading them on. And now it's too late to get rid of them."

"Why did you court them?"

She didn't really want Geoff to know how shallow she had been. He couldn't understand that she went from being a gawky, awkward teen to a beautiful woman overnight. And the attention was heady. Once she realized that it also garnered her father's attention, she'd been unable to resist.

"I thought—that's a lie. I didn't think at all. I just lapped it up like anyone else who gets some fame after years of being overlooked. It was like a drug and I was addicted. But then things got out of control."

She thought about that YouTube video—she was topless on her yacht with several of her mother's male models. It practically looked like she was orchestrating an orgy.

After that incident, she'd known she was going to have to take control of the media. She'd learned how to use them. They wanted something salacious so they'd get paid, and she needed her name in the headlines so that when she wanted to shine a spotlight on a cause, she could get the attention she needed.

"It's very convenient to have my little media hounds with me. They follow me to Africa when I go, and I get some pictures of the real plight over there back in the papers here. It's a trade-off and right now it's worth it."

"That's a very wise strategy," he said.

"I'm not known for being wise."

"That might be because most people are fooled by the smoke and mirrors. It takes a lot of smarts to keep the world believing you are nothing more than an empty-headed heiress, doesn't it?"

She shrugged. "Don't make me out to be a saint. I do love a good party and a good time. It's simply that at some point, we all have to grow up. And when I did, I looked around and realized that the only real assets I had were my family money and the media who follow me around."

He lifted his wineglass toward her. "You are definitely my kind of woman."

She lifted her glass and took a sip of her wine. She wasn't sure why but hearing him call her his kind of woman sent a little thrill through her entire body. She wanted to pretend that he didn't matter, that he was a guy just like all the others, but tonight had proven to be so much more than just a getting-to-know-you kind of date. Tonight had shown her that he thought of her as someone worth spending time with, someone he wanted to do business with, someone he felt he could trust. And it terrified her.

Geoff paid the bill and then escorted Amelia out of the restaurant. He knew that he'd gambled by going out with her tonight but despite his reputation for putting family and duty first, he was a man who seldom denied himself the finer things in life. Amelia Munroe was definitely one of the finer things in his life.

He put his hand on the small of her back as they walked out of the restaurant. Her hips swayed with each step she took and he couldn't help but admire her figure.

She glanced over her shoulder at him, her eyes smoldering with the same desire as his. Apparently she liked the feel of his hand on her. Almost as much as he liked touching her. No matter that she was still an enigma to him, that she wasn't what he had expected, that she hadn't exactly accepted his business proposal. He needed her. He needed her in his bed and he wanted to know all her secrets.

He wanted to be the man who made her forget her public persona, her family concerns, her work. And no matter what the cost, he was going to have her.

"Amelia, over here!"

"Who's the mystery man?"

"Devonshire, give her a kiss!"

The calls continued. Geoff ignored the paparazzi as he always did—he'd barely ever given them a chance to get a good photo of him. He signaled the valet to bring his car and when it arrived, he—not the valet—held open the door for Amelia.

"Come on, Amelia. Give us something we can use," one of the men said.

She smiled up at Geoff. In that instant, he realized how luscious her lips were. All evening he'd kept his mind on the conversation by looking straight in her eyes, but now he was failing miserably. All he wanted was to taste her, to know what it felt like to feel her lips against his. And he didn't give a damn who saw them. She stood up on tiptoe and wrapped her arms around his shoulders. He leaned down, intending to give her just a buss on the mouth, but he couldn't.

Their lips brushed and he felt an electric pulse down his body straight to his groin. He wanted to groan but controlled himself. Instead, he wrapped his hand in the hair at the back of her neck and tugged gently so he could take control of the kiss.

He plunged his tongue deep into her mouth. Her taste was addictive. He couldn't lift his head—not yet. He wanted more of her. Her lips were full and soft, and that expressive mouth that he'd watched all evening was finally his.

There were catcalls and whistles. Finally he came back to himself, remembering where they were. But he didn't give a damn about any of that. He wanted to be alone with Amelia so he could keep exploring her.

He lifted his head and looked down into her wide, dazed eyes. Her lips were shiny and swollen from his kisses. For a brief moment, he thought he had her, that he'd finally figured out how to master her. But she turned her head to the photographers and blew them a kiss before getting into the car. She was amazing, completely unpredictable. Dangerous.

He walked around the front of his car and seated himself, pulling away from the photographers calmly, though his gut instinct was to put the pedal to the floor.

Amelia made him forget the rules he always lived by, made him forget that he'd always tried to escape scandal by living above reproach. For once in his life, he didn't give a damn about that.

"You are a dangerous man, Geoff Devonshire," she said.

He spared a glance for her as he downshifted and saw that she held her fingers to her lips. She was staring pensively out the windshield and he wondered if she was playing a game that was getting out of control.

"If you play me like that again, you will regret it."

"I already do," she said. "You make it too easy to forget my own rules."

He almost laughed, and refrained from commenting on how similar they were.

"I'm surprised you'd admit that."

"Why wouldn't I? It's the truth. I don't think we should see each other again," she said.

"Like hell we shouldn't," he replied. "I'm not letting you go yet."

"I think I have some say in the matter," she said dryly.

He put his hand on her arm, feeling the shiver that went through her body.

"You are no more ready to walk away from me than I am from you. We have unfinished business," he said. "And if you want to lie and pretend that we don't, you are welcome to try, but your body is telling me a different story."

She reached over to his thigh and ran her fingers up the inside of his leg. He felt the lightest touch of her fingers against his erection and shuddered. He wanted her hands on his naked flesh. He wanted his mouth all over her naked body.

"You're right," she said in a low husky voice that made him even harder.

"Then we're agreed."

"Agreed?"

"That this isn't going to end until I'm buried hilt-deep in your sexy little body."

"Geoff, I'm not sure that's a good idea."

He pulled off the road, onto the lay-by, stopped the car and leaned across the gearshift. He took what he needed and gave what she wanted, kissing her until he felt as if he were going to explode if he couldn't explore more than her mouth.

When he lifted his head, she was breathing heavily and her hands were on his shoulders, trying to draw him back to her. She stared up at him with lust in her eyes and just a hint of panic that made him wonder if this was a mistake.

But it was too late now—there was no turning back. Amelia Munroe was going to be his and they both knew it.

Four

The kiss was beyond anything that Amelia had expected. Her body responded with ferocity and she had no say in the matter. Mr. Darcy had nothing on Geoff Devonshire when it came to sex appeal. He pulled the car back onto the highway and she realized she had no idea where they were going.

"Where are you taking me?" she asked. "I didn't even realize we'd left London proper."

"I'm taking an easier route. I was planning to take you home, unless you had something else in mind. I'd love to take you flying."

"Not tonight," she said. "What did you think I'd have in mind? I don't have an exotic love nest in the country, if that's what you're asking."

"Which wouldn't exactly be exotic," he said.

"I think I've just proved my point."

"Which is what, precisely?" he asked with a smile.

She shrugged. "I guess that I'm not what you might think."

"Love, I discovered that last night," he said. There was a kind and gentle note to his words that warmed her.

"Last night I thought you were a bit of a…"

"Prick?"

She laughed. Dammit, life would be a lot easier if Geoff were a jerk. "Maybe, but you did redeem yourself tonight."

"Did I?" he asked. "How? By kissing you?"

She didn't say anything for a few minutes. When she didn't like the way a conversation was going, she simply stopped it. It was avoidance, pure and simple, but she found that it was her only option. Her defenses disappeared around this man and it made her feel lost.

"Tell me."

"You're very bossy. I suspect it's because you're an older brother."

"Perhaps. But rumor has it I was bossy even before the girls came along."

"Truly? How interesting."

"Is your brother bossy?" he asked. He took the exit that led to her Hyde Park apartment.

"Auggie? No, he's demanding but that's not the same as bossy."

"No, it isn't. I have been called demanding as well," he said.

She could see that. Geoff was refined and very polite, but there was that underlying will in him that said he liked to have things his way. Like the way he'd kissed her. He had taken no prisoners and left her a mass of aching need. She wasn't used to that in the least, but she didn't mind it—in fact, his aggressive nature was becoming quite a turn-on. He wasn't the kind of man she could run circles around, like most of the others. Geoff would always want to be in charge and for once in her life, she was ready to loosen the reins a little.

"I'm a bit bossy at times myself," she confessed.

"More than a bit. The last meeting we had at your foundation, I heard you barking orders like the CEO of a major corporation."

"So if I tell you to drop and give me twenty…?"

"I'll drop and give you twenty of whatever you want, Amelia."

She felt her face flush and the ache in her body intensified. She couldn't think about anything but getting his lips on her again as they approached the high-rise apartment building she lived in.

"Want to come up?"

"I'd love to," he said.

"You can leave your car in the garage," she said.

He parked in one of the spots reserved for guests and then came around to open her door. When he reached down to offer her his hand, she had butterflies in her stomach. Geoff was different—something about him practically made her feel like a nervous schoolgirl. Granted, she wasn't used to such gentlemanly behavior. She knew she wasn't going to have to worry about him wanting her to do something kinky so he could brag about it to his friends. Guys like that she could handle because she knew exactly what to expect from them—they were a dime a dozen. But not Geoff.

Her imagination began to run away with her. She was hoping that in the morning he'd still be in her bed. And they'd wake up together and have breakfast.

No, she thought. *I'd better get a hold of myself before this gets way out of hand and I show him too much.*

She used her key card to activate the elevator in the main building. Geoff kept his hand on the small of her back as they waited. His fingers were fanned out and he made a small circle with his index finger that made her entire lower body start to pulse.

"You didn't have to invite me up," he said.

"I know."

A few years ago, after the video turned up on YouTube and she'd been hounded by men who assumed she was kinky, she'd established a new rule for herself—no sex on the first date. But she wasn't sure she was going to be able to stick to that rule tonight.

A part of her believed that if she didn't do it now, she might never be brave enough to let him this close again. She knew tomorrow she'd have regrets that stemmed from letting him see too much of the woman she was.

She'd have to find a way to put distance between them again, to convince him that she was just an heiress who liked a lot of attention. And the only way to do that was to take what she wanted tonight and walk away tomorrow.

But that was tomorrow. Tonight he was hers and she vowed to enjoy every second.

Amelia's penthouse was an eclectic mix of classical and modern styles. She had sleek Japanese tables and plush Italian leather sofas in her living area. The floor-to-ceiling wall of glass that overlooked London allowed the viewer to see all the way to Buckingham Palace.

On the wall was a large Monet from the artist's time in Argenteuil. On another wall was a painting of Amelia done in the Andy Warhol "Marilyn Monroe" style, with four of the same images in different colors.

Her small dog bounded out of the bedroom as soon as she'd walked in the door.

"How's my Lady Godiva?" Amelia asked, bending over to pet her dog.

The miniature Dachshund stood on her back legs with her tail wagging. Amelia scooped the little dog up and brought her over toward him.

"This is Lady Godiva. Godiva, this is Geoff," Amelia said.

He scratched the dog under her chin. Amelia set the dog down. "Go to bed," she commanded.

The little dog trotted off to a large pillow in the corner and circled around several times before lying down.

"Impressive," Geoff said.

Amelia smiled. "Would you like a drink?" she asked.

"Yes," he said.

She went to a wet bar in the corner and reached under the counter. "Cognac?"

"I'd enjoy one."

She gestured toward the sofa. "You can have a seat over there, or if you'd like, the stairs in the corner lead to my rooftop garden."

"I'll wait for you," he said.

She took out two large snifters and warmed them in her hands before pouring in a generous portion of the dark-colored liquor. She carried the drinks over to where he waited. He was watching her closely and she felt the butterflies fluttering again.

She handed him a drink and they toasted.

"To this evening."

"To us," she said. "I think the garden will be nice tonight, since it's not raining and not too cloudy. Want to give it a try?"

"I'd love to."

She led the way to her sanctuary, knowing full well that it was only a matter of time before her need would get the better of her.

He followed her up the wrought-iron staircase that was in the corner of the living room. She climbed up steadily in her high heels. He tried to do the gentlemanly thing and not stare up her skirt as she climbed but it was hard to resist looking. After all, he'd been thinking about what was under her skirt all night.

The cognac was good but it didn't taste as addictive as her mouth. He wanted to taste her again. But since they'd entered her apartment she'd been keeping her distance, and he was going to let her have all the space she needed. It was enough that he was here with her.

She opened the door to the rooftop garden and stepped out into the night. He followed her, breathing in the heavy air. It was crisp and cool, and smelled like spring. There was a hint of rain but also the scent of blooming flowers.

She hit a button on the wall and small lights lit up the area. A fountain started filling the night with the gentle sound of flowing water. He looked around the garden oasis that he was standing in—from here it was hard to tell he was in the middle of one of the busiest cities in the world.

"I like this."

"I'm glad. I needed a place to escape to when I couldn't get away so I created this area."

"You created it?"

"I did all the work except the heavy lifting. I figured if it was going to be my retreat I didn't want anyone else up here. If I had workers helping, they'd sell the story to some paper and then I wouldn't have any peace."

He stepped closer to her and rubbed the back of her neck. Her life did take a toll on her, clearly. And he didn't want to add to the stress.

"I'm honored that you are sharing it with me."

"Count yourself lucky. I don't let just anyone up here."

"Why me?"

"You're different," she said, closing her eyes for a moment as his fingers stroked her neck and shoulders. Then she pulled away and walked toward the bench nestled in the trees near the fountain.

He followed her slowly. Amelia was different here in her garden. She wouldn't look directly at him, and it struck him that she was vulnerable.

She'd invited him to the place where she let down her guard and he wondered if she had second thoughts now.

"This is the second secret you've shown me tonight."

"What was the first?" she asked, looking at him carefully.

"That you are more than the shallow socialite. This is the real Amelia Munroe, and I feel very privileged that you brought me here."

"Come sit with me."

"Are you sure?"

She nodded.

He did as she asked. The bench was a solid wrought-iron frame with a thick padded cushion. He sipped his cognac and wrapped an arm around her.

"Do you wish you hadn't invited me up here?"

She shook her head and the silky strands of her thick hair brushed against his neck as she turned her face toward him.

"I'm not sure what to do now. With anyone else I'd be a little drunk and I wouldn't be thinking so much."

He wondered how often she drank simply to endure her life or merely because it was expected of her. He suddenly felt the need to protect her, shield her from what the world expected her to be.

"Really?"

She shrugged. "In the old days. I haven't brought a guy home in a long time."

He arched an eyebrow at her. "You've been seen with men lately."

"You and I both know that being *seen* with someone has nothing to do with actually *being* with someone."

He took their glasses and put them on the ground by their feet. Then he took her beautiful face in his hands, rubbing his thumb over the blade of her cheek and down to the full curve of her bottom lip.

"That's very true," he said, leaning in for the kiss that he felt like he'd waited ages to claim.

It wasn't the dramatic, lust-filled kiss he'd given her in front of the restaurant. It was deep and steady, and made promises that he wasn't ready to vocalize but that he couldn't help making with his lips. This woman was special and he wanted her in his arms for a very long time.

Amelia knew that inviting Geoff to her place wasn't the wisest decision she had ever made, but she didn't regret it. She'd had learned fairly early on that if she was going to be able to live in her own skin she couldn't regret anything. She'd have to just learn from it and move on.

Being in Geoff's arms felt too good for her to think about regrets. His hands skimmed up and down her back and she shivered with awareness as his mouth moved over hers.

He was touching her with such skill and tenderness that her head was spinning. He was passionate. And commanding. Everything that he was in business she realized he was in life.

She'd made a mistake in judging him. The way he'd probably made a mistake in judging her.

What if he expected something exotic from her? Thanks to the media's interpretation of the video that ended up on YouTube, past lovers had expected some strange things from her.

She pulled back. "Did you see that video?"

He stared down at her, his brooding eyes unreadable, and she wondered if this would be the moment that he left. Was this going to be the one thing that would make him think poorly of her?

Why had she brought it up?

"I haven't. I'm not the kind of man who bothers with things like that."

"Oh, well, it was a long time ago. I mean I know that everyone thinks it just happened yesterday but I was a lot younger."

She was babbling. She couldn't help it. Every part of her was outraged that the video had been shared the way it had. She hated that everyone thought they knew intimate details about her because of one mistake.

"Amelia, love, you don't have to explain anything. I've done things in my past that I wouldn't want the world to watch online. What you and I share together has nothing to do with a video."

He kissed her so softly and tenderly then that she almost wept. She felt like he was truly kissing her, Amelia, not some idea or expectation of her.

He was healing a part of her she hadn't realized needed to be healed. She wrapped her arms around his shoulders and tunneled her fingers into the thick hair at the nape of his neck. She held him to her, realizing in that moment that she didn't want him to let her go.

She needed this more than she'd expected. When his mouth moved over hers and his hands explored her body she didn't care about the what-ifs—she didn't want to think about tomorrow or about consequences. She just wanted to feel.

She touched the buttons at the top of his shirt and undid them while he caressed her from shoulder blade to breast and back again. He found the zipper in the side of her dress and drew it down slowly. Every caress seemed to last longer than the first. And the feel of his hands on her body was an exquisite torture that she couldn't get enough of.

She reached for the neckline of her dress, wanting the fabric out of the way so that she could feel his hands on her flesh, but he stopped her.

"Not so fast. I wish to savor you."

She shivered at the note of lust in his voice. No one had ever wanted to make slow love to her before.

"I want your hands on me."

"They are," he said, running his hands down her back, spanning her waist and bringing them back to her front.

She realized that he wasn't going to be hurried. He would take his time until he drove her insane with pleasure. Two can play at this game, she thought, reaching for the buttons of his shirt again and undoing the rest of them.

She pushed the fabric open and finally had her hands on his chest. It was well muscled and lightly dusted with hair. She ran her fingers from his neck to his waistband, following the line of his sternum. She lightly scraped her nails down his chest and he shuddered as her touch moved over his abdomen.

"Do you like that?"

"Yes," he growled.

She smiled to herself as she reached lower, stroking his erection through the fabric of his pants. He grew harder and longer under her fingers as she found his zipper. But instead of lowering it, she simply stroked him harder through his pants. His hips shifted, following her touch, and she leaned forward to kiss his chest.

He smelled so good. She took a deep breath of

his unique scent—she'd never smelled anything so wonderful in her entire life.

His hands were back on her body, slipping inside the opening of her dress and finding the clasp of her bra between her shoulder blades. He kept one hand there, splayed across her back as he drew her forward. The other hand pulled the loosened dress away from her body.

"Take your arms out of this dress," he said, his voice shot through with desire.

She followed his commands. He pushed the bodice of her dress and her bra straps down until she was naked from the waist up. The night air caressed her bare skin as she studied his face.

He held her wrists loosely in both hands and stared down at her. She wondered if she was pleasing to him—every man liked something different in a woman's body. She hoped he got as much pleasure from looking at her as she did from seeing him.

He brought his free hand up to her mouth and touched her lips before drawing one finger down her body. He traced the line of her collarbone and then moved lower. His fingers fanned out to caress her chest and then the full globes of her breasts.

Her nipples tightened and she wanted to feel his fingers on them. She shifted her shoulders but again she was reminded that he wouldn't be hurried. When he could tell she liked what he was doing, he seemed to slow his pace even more, making her whole body ache with desire.

His hands spread down her back, bringing her forward until the tips of her nipples brushed against his chest.

She shivered as her blood began to run heavier. He held her firmly in his arms, making very sure that she stayed where he wanted her to. She tipped her head back and met his dark blue eyes.

"Are you sure this is what you want?" he asked her.

She couldn't really think—all she could do was feel and every atom of her being cried out for Geoff. She nodded.

"You have to say it. Before this goes any further, do you want me, Amelia?"

She reached up and cupped his strong jaw in both her hands. Then she leaned in and spoke her words against his lips.

"Yes, Geoff. I want you."

Five

Geoff had never held a woman like Amelia. She made him feel alive in a way that he had never experienced before. And now he was going to claim her for his own. A part of him felt that she was already his, that he wouldn't feel this strongly about a woman who wasn't meant to be in his arms.

He took control of the soft kiss she had initiated and brought his hands to her nipples at the same time. She moaned in the back of her throat, inflaming him even more.

He teased her with soft touches at first, running the pads of his fingers over her aureole. Then, when he felt her nipple bead under his finger, he scraped her lightly with his nail.

She tightened her hands on his shoulders and

pulled her mouth from his. Her head fell back and he hesitated.

"Do you like that?" he asked, wanting to be sure that he wasn't hurting her.

"Yessss."

He continued to caress her breasts and brought his mouth down the side of her jaw. He dropped nibbling kisses on her neck and when he reached the base of it, he suckled gently right over her pulse.

She came alive then. Her hands grasped him and her body moved over his until she straddled him. Her skirt pulled taut at her knees and she moaned in frustration.

He slid his hands under the skirt of her dress, pulling it up to her waist. She wore only a minute pair of bikini panties and he slipped his hands under them to cup her buttocks.

He moved one hand forward and felt the humid warmth at her center. He could no longer resist, rubbing one finger up and down her slit over her panties until she was moaning his name.

"What do you want?" he asked, whispering in her ear.

She shivered and shifted her body against his hand, trying to increase the strength of each stroke of her feminine center.

"You. Geoff, I want you."

"Not yet," he said, carefully moving her panties to the side so he could touch her bare flesh.

She made a soft sound when he touched her skin. He tugged harder on her panties and ripped the delicate fabric from her body.

"You owe me…"

"I'm going to give you an orgasm to make up for it," he said.

She gasped at his blunt words and a flush spread across her face.

He smiled to himself. He'd never had a woman whose passion matched his as perfectly as Amelia's did. She reached between them, grasped his zipper and freed his erection.

He felt the warmth of her center spilling over on him—it made him so hot and hard, he felt as if he would explode at any second.

But he wasn't ready to come yet.

He wanted her to have so much pleasure that she'd be addicted to him the way he was quickly becoming addicted to her.

"I have to tell you I'm unprepared," he confessed. He hadn't brought a condom with him since he hadn't anticipated this ending to the evening. "Are you protected?"

"Yes, I am," she said.

"Thank God."

She laughed. "Why, would you have been upset if we'd had to stop?"

He took both of her nipples in his hands and pinched lightly. She moaned and moved against him, her slit sliding over his erection.

"I don't think I could have handled that."

"Take me, Geoff. Make me yours."

He shifted his hips until the tip of his penis was at the entrance to her body, but he held still.

"Once you are mine there is no going back," he said.

"What do you mean?"

"This isn't a one-time thing. I'm not like the other men you've dated."

"This isn't the time for a conversation," she said, groaning, rubbing herself against him.

He put his hands on her hips and started to draw her forward as he thrust up into her body. She was tight, fitting around him like a velvet glove. She squeezed him so tightly that he had to stop and breathe to keep from spilling himself with just one stroke.

He held her hips as she tried to move and set about bringing her to the brink. He bent and caught the tip of her breast in his mouth. His tongue teased her nipple and he used the very edge of his teeth on her until she was clutching at his shoulders and frantically trying to move her hips in his hands.

He heard her long moan and then felt the minute tightening of her inner muscles as an orgasm ripped through her body. Only then did he let go of her hips and thrust up into her with all his strength. He took her mouth as he felt that telltale tingling at the bottom of his spine.

His orgasm was coming and he looked up into her eyes to find them half opened. He knew she was on the verge of coming again. He reached between their bodies and found the center of her pleasure, stroking her until he heard those sexy gasping sounds again that made him want to explode.

"Come for me," he said.

She did. He came a moment later, spilling himself inside her. He wrapped his arms around her back as she collapsed against his chest. He held her tight, resting his head on top of hers and realizing that he didn't know if he was ever going to be able to let her go.

Amelia couldn't catch her breath and didn't want to. Geoff's arms around her were solid and he held her close, as if she might disappear if he didn't. She loved it. She had wanted to find a man who would make her feel cherished for as long as she could remember, and it might be self-delusion, but right now, she felt cherished.

She felt Geoff sliding out of her body and the sweat on his chest was starting to dry, but he continued to hold her. She stayed where she was with her face resting against his neck and forgot that there was a world outside his arms.

The longer he held her, the more reluctant she was to actually get up. But she knew she couldn't stay in his arms forever. So she made herself do it.

She lifted her head, intent on disentangling herself from him. But he kissed her when she looked down at him. It was a soft, gentle kiss but she could still feel the passion that had flared between them.

"Where do you think you're going?" he said.

"I just need a second," she answered, suddenly feeling very exposed. This was much more than that fragile emotion she'd experienced when she'd brought him into her home for the first time. This was too intense. She had no idea what to do or say next.

She wanted him to stay—wanted to spend the night in his arms—but this was a first date. Dammit, this was another reason why sex on the first date was a mistake. If you truly cared about the person, things could get very complicated very quickly.

She used his shoulders for balance, climbed off his lap and stood next to the bench. Her dress started to fall to the ground but he caught it as he stood up and helped her with it. He wrapped one big arm around her shoulders and kissed her again. He kept her tucked under his arm.

"Shall we go back inside then?" he said.

She nodded. He reached down, tucking himself in his pants and fastening just the button. Then he lifted her into his arms.

"What are you doing?"

"Carrying you," he said.

"Why?"

"Because I'm not ready to let go of you yet."

He carried her down the stairs into her apartment. She gave him directions to the master en suite bathroom and he set her on her feet next to the sink. The bathroom was large and luxurious, something she'd insisted on when she'd had it designed.

"Would you care for a bath?" he asked.

"Geoff, you are going to spoil me."

"It's the least I can do. I did ruin your panties," he said.

She flushed, remembering how the sound of the ripping fabric had made her so wanton in his arms. "Yes, you did."

He adjusted the taps on the large tub and let the water run. She stepped out of her dress as Geoff quietly undressed next to her. She opened a jar of bath salts and poured a small scoop into the warm water.

She turned on the towel-warming rack and got an extra towel out for him. As silly as it sounded, she'd never bathed with another person before. Geoff seemed at home, though, and that put her at ease. He held her hand and helped her into the tub, then climbed in after her.

He settled himself back against the wall and drew her down so that her back was pressed to his chest. Then he took the loofah sponge she had on the tray next to the bathtub and poured some bath gel onto it. Her skin tingled in anticipation.

"Tell me more about growing up. How did you become a world-famous heiress?"

She tipped her head back against his shoulder and looked up at him, trying to see if he was teasing her, but his expression was sincere. "I think I'm more infamous."

"No, you aren't," he said. "Tell me."

"What do you know about me?" she asked. "I take it you don't want the story of my birth."

He laughed, a deep rumbling sound that echoed off the bathroom walls. "No, I don't. I know your father is Augustus Munroe and your mother is Mia Domenici, the legendary fashion designer."

"My father was married when he met my mother, but they have what she calls 'fiery passion,' and that, apparently, is something that can never be denied."

"It can't?" Geoff asked.

She shook her head, realizing that she understood now what her mother had meant. She'd never experienced passion like it until Geoff. Why him? What draws people to each other in such an extreme way? She was sure her own mother wondered why Gus Munroe had inspired that kind of passion in her.

"Have you experienced it?" he asked.

"Only once," she said. She didn't want to reveal that she was thinking of him, of what had just happened between them. She had no idea what this all meant to him. Perhaps she was just another woman to pass the time with until he found someone suitable to be his wife.

He stroked the sponge over her body. She knew she shouldn't want him again so soon but every time the sponge brushed over her breasts she felt an answering pulse between her legs.

"Have you experienced it?" she asked him.

"Define it for me," he said.

She shrugged. She didn't know how to put it into words without revealing that he was the man who'd inspired it in her. She really hoped that her affair with Geoff didn't turn out as disastrously as her parents' relationship had. Despite their marriage, they had never found the happily-ever-after that Amelia wanted for herself. She wondered if passion precluded happiness.

She hoped not.

"I don't really know how to put it into words. I only know that in my parents' case, it wasn't enough. They need each other desperately but can't live together."

"Sounds painful. Did you understand that as a child?"

She shook her head. "No I didn't. Auggie and I often felt as if we were on a sailboat in the rough sea, trying desperately to keep ourselves from capsizing."

Amelia had the sensation once again that she was revealing way too much. She decided to close her eyes—and her mouth—and revel in the feel of his touch, however long it lasted.

Geoff wanted to protect Amelia but she was a woman who had always scorned the protection of others, hadn't she? That had been his impression. Listening to her talk about her childhood, however, made him believe that she'd always had to make her own way and figure everything out on her own.

"I don't remember seeing much of you in the papers when you were a child," he said vaguely, fishing for information from her. He already knew that if he demanded it she'd simply clam up and tell him nothing.

"I spent most of my childhood in New York, but frankly, they weren't at all interested in me until I turned eighteen. I'm afraid to say I was a bit of an ugly duckling."

"There's no way I could believe that," he said.

She lifted one of her delicate shoulders. "Well, I was. I had braces and glasses. I was just about as awkward as a young girl can get, much to my father's great disappointment."

She was rambling a little and he realized she did that when she was nervous. "I'm sure you were lovely."

She shook her head. "You say that now but if you had met me back then, you wouldn't have even noticed me."

"That's where you're wrong," he said. "I have two sisters. If you were half as awkward as they were, I would have gone over to talk to you just to let you know you weren't alone."

She looked up at him, those wide weary eyes of hers trying to see if he was telling the truth. He hoped she could read the sincerity in his eyes. "So you became a sexy young woman and the paparazzi just swarmed around you?"

She laughed, a very sweet sound that made him want to hug her closer.

"Not exactly. I wore a very sexy dress that my mother had designed for me to my then-boyfriend's film premiere. And when they took photos of Andy and me, people started asking who I was. And Andy told them. We went to a few more functions together and then we broke up. But the paparazzi were still following me and at the time, I liked it. And so did my parents—it kept the family name in the public eye."

Andy was Andrew Hollings, one of the hottest directors in Hollywood. She lived in the world of celebrity and for a second, he wondered how a British peer measured up. But based on the way she'd responded to him, he didn't think he'd been found wanting.

He and Amelia were electric together. He had thought maybe there was fiery passion between them because of that addictive thing he felt for her. But he supposed it was just the newness of lust that made him feel that way.

He finished washing her, feeling himself harden as he touched her. He wanted her again. And he knew he'd take her another time tonight.

But not now. He wanted to know more about Amelia than how her body reacted to his touch. He wanted to know the secrets behind her eyes. He needed to find out every detail of her past and present.

Damn, he was obsessed.

How had that happened? It was sometime between the restaurant and here. Probably when she'd taken him out on her rooftop garden and shown him her own private hideaway—and let him into her luscious body. He struggled to focus.

"Is that when you decided to use the paparazzi?" he asked.

"This is going to make me sound like a spoiled brat, but please keep in mind that I was young and not very mature," she said.

"I will."

"Every time I had a photo in the papers or showed up on TV, my father would call me. I was speaking to him more than I had in my entire life. And though the conversations weren't meaningful, I finally had his attention."

"And you weren't about to give it up," Geoff concluded.

"That's right. I don't know what your relationship is with your parents, but I was largely forgotten. Auggie and Dad were close because they play polo together. But Mom was always in Milan and I was not very… fashionable, so I didn't fit in."

He suspected that having been left alone so much of the time was one of the reasons she was able to project such a strong sense of self—one of the many qualities that made her attractive to the public.

"Were you lonely?"

"A little, but not too much. I was at boarding school and then camps for most of the year. And my friend Bebe always invited me home with her for holidays."

"My childhood was similar," he said. "Except I was usually the one inviting mates home for the holidays."

"I don't know a lot about your upbringing. Caroline and Gemma are your half sisters?"

"Yes. My mother is Princess Louisa and my father is Malcolm Devonshire. They never married."

"I did know that. I heard that you and your half brothers were summoned to Malcolm's office by that attorney of his, Edmond. Is that an odd occurrence?"

"Do you know Edmond?" Geoff asked, surprised.

"I know of him," she replied. "He's one of my mother's friend's lawyers."

Geoff didn't want to talk about his brothers, but he couldn't continue to ignore her question. "It was the first time we'd met in person."

"That's odd. Why?"

"I'm not sure exactly. My mother is very sensitive to the subject of Malcolm's other sons, so I never brought up anything about them."

She turned in his arms to face him. "I'm sorry."

"Why?"

"Because that means you had no brothers to share with, to tell what was going on in your life. I don't imagine you had a close confidant as I did in Bebe."

"I had my half sisters eventually," he said. "I have a good life."

"I know. But you still missed out on that ideal childhood that everyone craves."

"Everyone?"

"Yes, we all pretend it doesn't matter that we didn't have our parents' attention but we all know it does. Our crazy childhoods shaped us into the adults we are."

She was wise, this sexy little heiress of his. He kissed her to get her mind out of the past and back in the present. He didn't want to admit that she might be right. He didn't want to give Malcolm any more control over his life than the man already had.

And when he had a naked Amelia in his arms he wanted to be focused on her and he wanted her attention on him. "I'm tired of talking."

"What do you want to do?" she asked, wrapping those long fingers around his head and pulling him down for a long, lingering kiss.

"I have a few ideas," he said in a growl.

"Do you?"

"Indeed," he said. "Why don't you show me your bedroom?"

He wrapped a warm towel around her and picked her up again, carrying her into the bedroom. He set her on the center of the bed and came down on top of her.

Six

Geoff woke to the sound of his mobile phone ringing. He reached for the device on his bedside table and hit a glass of water that spilled everywhere. He jerked upright in bed.

He was at Amelia's. She had propped herself up on one arm and was staring at him through a mass of tangled curly hair. Her lips were swollen and the sheet fell to her waist, baring her breasts. He forgot about the ringing phone and the water. Instead, he reached forward and touched her, running his finger down the centerline of her body and around her breasts.

"You're gorgeous."

She blushed and he saw that the color started just above her breasts and went up over her face. He leaned down to kiss her when his mobile phone started ringing again.

"Get that," she said in an amused tone.

He reached for his phone. "I spilled some water."

"I'll take care of it," she said.

He had managed not to knock the water over onto his phone. He glanced at the caller ID and saw that it was his mother.

"Hi, Mum."

"Geoff, we need to talk."

"Is it about the party? I already spoke to Caro. No one is going to follow me to Hampshire. The paparazzi are content to follow Henry around—he's the one who lives a life worthy of their headlines."

"Not anymore, darling. Have you seen *The Sun* today?"

"No," he said. "I don't normally read it." If his mother was asking about the paper, that could only mean one thing. "Is there a picture of Caro and that footballer she's dating?"

"No, Geoff, there isn't. There's a photo of you with Amelia Munroe. And I have to say you are giving them a lot to talk about."

"Mum—"

"Don't. Don't say anything. You can't justify your actions by saying that a girl like that is used to the attention."

"I wouldn't say that."

"Good. Because even socialites have feelings, Geoff. Every woman deserves to be treated with respect. Are you going to see her again?"

"Mum, I don't want to discuss this with you."

"Are you still at her place?" his mother asked.

"As I said, I don't want to discuss this."

"Make sure she understands where you stand. Don't lead her on, Geoff."

This was probably as close as he and his mother were ever going to get to discussing how she'd felt when it had been revealed that Malcolm had been dating two other women while he had been wooing her. "I would never do that. Amelia is different."

"Than who?"

"Everyone," he said.

Amelia had come back into the room. He did want to protect her from the scandal that the media attention could bring, but in this case, he guessed she might be better at dealing with it than he was. He would ignore it and the stories would go away. But for Amelia it was a way of life.

"I want to talk to you about this later. Why don't you bring her to dinner this weekend at your place in Bath?"

"I'll call you later. I love you, Mum."

"I love you, too, but we aren't finished with this."

He hung up and took Amelia's arm, drawing her down onto his side of the bed. He pulled her head down to his and kissed her. "Good morning."

"Is it good?" she asked.

"Indeed. It's very good," he said. He wrapped both arms around her, intent on making love to her before he went anywhere this morning. But his mobile phone rang again.

"You are one popular man. Why don't you answer that while I make us some coffee?" she asked. She walked naked across the room to the armoire and removed a pale blue dressing gown, which she wrapped around her body.

"How do you take your coffee?"

"Black," he said.

"I'll be right back."

"You don't have to leave," he said.

She raised a brow at him. "Yes, I do. They are all calling about me, right?"

"It's probably one of my sisters. The photo of our kiss is apparently in *The Sun* this morning."

She wrapped her arms around her waist in a defensive posture. Instantly, she seemed miles away from him. "That's nothing new for me. Are you okay?"

"Sure. There isn't anything to the story. It will fade away in a few days."

"It will?" she asked.

"Of course. I've found that if I don't give them anything to print, they grow bored with me and move on to something else."

She nodded. "I'll go get the coffee started."

She walked away and he could tell that something wasn't right. He had said something that had upset her.

He got out of bed, leaving his ringing mobile phone on the table, and padded naked to her kitchen. She was leaning against the counter staring at the granite surface as if it held a mystery she had to figure out. But when she sensed him, she busied herself with putting dog food in a bowl for Godiva and filling up her water dish. She set them both on a mat on the floor.

"Talk to me, Amelia. Tell me why you're upset," he said.

She looked at him, biting her lip for a moment. Then she shrugged. "I was hoping you and I would last longer than one night," she said. "But I guess we can't. We'd be all over the news constantly, and I know how much you'd hate that."

He pulled her into his arms and kissed her long and hard. He wasn't ready to walk away and he sure as hell wasn't going to let her walk away, either.

"When I said the story would fade in a few days, I meant *the press* would lose interest, Amelia, not that *I* would. I couldn't lose interest now if my life depended on it. We'll just have to keep a low profile."

Amelia wasn't too sure she wanted to keep a low profile. If she vanished from the public eye, would she still have any influence? She had always lived her life by her own rules. Now she realized that if she was going to be with Geoff, she'd have to adapt.

"I don't know if I can," she admitted honestly.

"Are you willing to try?"

She pushed the button on her coffeepot and put her Van Gogh mug underneath the spout. She reached above her head and took down a matching one for Geoff.

She handed him the black coffee when it was ready and took a sip of her mocha latte.

"You are asking me to change the way I normally operate," she said.

"Is that too much? I think it's justified," he said.

Of course he would. He didn't need the media to make his life manageable to keep the family business running smoothly, to garner free publicity for his causes—and to make his father happy.

"I'll try," she said at last.

"That's all I ask," he said, moving to her and taking her in his arms.

"You are still naked," she mentioned.

"Does that turn you on?" he asked.

There was something playful about him this morning. She wanted to smile but she couldn't. She'd overheard enough of his conversation to know that his mother had been concerned about that photo. And she was sure that wasn't a good thing.

"Let's go back to bed."

She shook her head. "I can't. I have to go to the Munroe offices this morning."

"To fix the problems left by your brother?"

"Yes," she said.

"Have you given my proposition any thought?" he asked.

"I haven't exactly had my mind on business, now have I?" she replied as he kissed her neck.

Geoff took her by the hand, leading the way back into her bedroom.

She watched his tush as he walked in front her. He was one fine-looking man naked. He wasn't hard-bodied like a weight lifter but he was in shape and everything was perfectly proportioned. She reached for him, wanting to touch him, when he turned around.

"What are you doing?"

"Admiring your backside," she admitted, reaching around and cupping his butt. "You have a very nice one."

He flushed, which made her smile. "Should we talk

a little business, or should we talk about my bum some more?"

"What's your proposition again? I'm a little distracted right now."

"I propose that we do a joint business venture, maybe some luxury vacation packages that would partner Everest Air with the Munroe Hotels. It would distract the board from Auggie's issues and we'd get to spend a lot of time together."

"So we'd work on this together?"

"Indeed we would. In fact, I think we should meet about it right now."

"In my bed?" she asked.

"Yes."

"I'm being serious, Geoff."

"Me, too. Let me make love to you and then I'll take you to breakfast and we can discuss the details."

Standing in her bedroom with light streaming in from the tinted windows, she had a hard time saying no to him. She wanted to be in his arms, but she had no idea if she should entangle herself further or escape.

This morning she was making business deals and promises and she wasn't sure why. Hell, that was a lie. She knew why. Geoff was too much a man for her to let him go this soon.

For the first time, she'd met a man she wanted to spend more than one night with. She'd met a man she wanted to get to know better. She wanted to see if their lives would blend, if she could change the way she lived so they could be together.

She'd met a man who had the potential to make her fall in love with him. It was as simple as that.

That should be the warning signal, she thought. That one reason should send her running away. Instead, she found herself slipping her dressing gown off her shoulders and letting it fall to the floor.

She pushed against Geoff's chest and he walked backward to the bed. He fell back and pulled her down with him.

She straddled his body and kissed him as his hands came up to rove all over her back and down to her butt. He murmured sexy words into her ear, which turned her on.

He positioned himself at the entrance of her body and she felt just the tip of his erection inside her. She rocked her hips and took him all the way inside. He felt so right inside her that she could scarcely breathe.

Last night she'd thought it had just been the magic of their first time making love, but he still felt right. He wrapped his arms around her and rolled over in one swift motion so she was underneath him. He took her face in his hands and kissed her long and deep as his hips kept driving into her until she realized she was going to come.

It happened quickly, taking her by surprise. He smiled down at her as she gasped, then he started pumping faster into her. A minute later, he came with a deep groan. She wrapped her arms and legs around him and held him with a strength that she hoped he didn't notice.

She was in deep trouble. She already cared for Geoff. She already wanted him to stay by her side and be the man she'd always secretly wanted to find.

And she knew that if he disappointed her, she wasn't going to recover from it easily.

* * *

Geoff left Amelia's to go home and get showered and changed. They were going to meet at his office midmorning to discuss the joint venture. As he entered his house, it felt strangely empty to him and he realized that he wanted to bring her here. He wanted to see her in his home.

This was getting out of control. He was as randy as he'd been at eighteen and no matter how many times he had Amelia, he still wanted her again, as if it were the first time.

She enchanted him. There was no other word for it. He was caught completely in her web. Everything about her just made him want her more.

He was aware that he had to walk a fine line here, and handle mixing his personal and professional life with care. He would keep Amelia and himself out of the spotlight from now on. He could do that if she agreed to it. It would be important for their new venture to project the right image.

He checked his mobile phone as he got out of the shower and saw that he had two missed calls. One was from Caro—no doubt some warning about staying out of papers like *The Sun*. The other was from Edmond.

He returned Edmond's call first.

"This is Geoff Devonshire," he said when Edmond answered.

"Thank you for returning my call."

"Not a problem. What can I do for you?"

"I'm not sure if you've seen the morning papers, but there is a photo of you and Ms. Munroe in it."

Geoff wasn't used to answering to anyone for his

actions and he didn't expect to start now. "I have seen it. I don't think it's a problem."

"In fact, there is. Your father is not exactly interested in having his company associated with the likes of Ms. Munroe."

Geoff took a deep breath. "Then it's a good thing he has handed over Everest Air to me, isn't it, since it's mine to run."

"This is a warning, Geoff. If you continue to see Amelia Munroe, you will forfeit your piece of the Everest Company."

"I think you would do well to remember that I am already a successful man and don't exactly need Everest Air."

"Again, this is just a warning," Edmond said. "I don't want you to do anything you might regret. And judging by what I saw at the benefit between the two of you, and in the paper this morning, you are headed for disaster. Stay away from her if you want to keep Everest Air."

If there was one thing Geoff knew he wouldn't regret, it was spending time with Amelia. Images of last night flashed through his mind and he closed his eyes.

"I want to speak to you about the articles that Steven proposed we take part in," Geoff said, changing the subject. "I'm not sure that my mother will do it. She's spent her entire life making sure she wasn't ever linked to the other Devonshire mistresses."

"I am aware of that, but I think the publicity would be good for the company, and would help put the scandal in the past as you and your brothers take your places in the company. Do you think you can try to convince her?"

"I'll ask but she's very sensitive on this subject. If she says no, then that will have to be the answer."

"I understand. Do you need to meet this week to talk about Everest Air?"

"Not at all. I have some new ideas we will be implementing, and we have the baggage handler situation under control."

"Sounds like you are taking to running the airline just as your father hoped."

"Please don't refer to him as my father, Edmond. You and I both know that Malcolm was little more than a sperm donor."

"Of course," Edmond said.

Geoff knew the older man wanted to say more—he could hear it in Edmond's voice. But to him, Malcolm wasn't a father. He had a mother and two great sisters. His family was complete without Malcolm.

"If that's all."

"For now," Edmond said and hung up the phone.

Geoff put on his Hugo Boss suit with a dark blue striped shirt and a yellow tie. His handmade Italian loafers fit perfectly and before he walked out the door, he glanced in the mirror, turning around to look at his backside.

He shook his head. Just because Amelia said she liked it.

He put his mobile phone in his pocket. His housekeeper was just coming out of the kitchen as he walked in.

"Good morning, Mr. Devonshire," Annie said.

"Good morning. I will not be home for dinner tonight," he said. "Will you alert the chef?" On the nights when he was home for dinner, Annie made sure he had a hot meal waiting for him.

"Very well, sir. And this weekend?"

"I will be going out of town," he said. He wanted to take Amelia away from the city. "I need the house in Bath prepared."

"I will see to it. Do you need meals there?" she asked.

"Just make sure the kitchen is stocked and I will take care of it."

"You will?"

He arched one eyebrow at her.

"I'm just remembering the smoky mess the last time you 'took care of it,'" she said.

Annie was cheeky, which was why he liked her. She was his mother's age but still had a sparkle in her eyes and enjoyed life. "I was planning to grill."

"Good idea."

"I'm planning a house party so make sure we have enough food for at least ten," he said.

He left his home with the feeling that everything was right in his world, despite the warning from Edmond. He knew that at the end of the day no matter how much Edmond and Malcolm wanted him to avoid scandal, the bottom line would determine the winner of the Devonshire will. And he wasn't going to let anyone give him an ultimatum involving Amelia Munroe. He wanted her, and he sure as hell wasn't giving her up.

Seven

Amelia dressed in the classic Chanel black suit that put Coco on the map and walked out of her apartment building. She'd straightened her black hair into a classic Audrey Hepburn updo and put on a pair of large, round sunglasses.

She'd thought about this outfit long and hard before leaving her apartment, trying to come up with the perfect elegant, low-key ensemble. She breezed past Tommy at the entrance, feeling like a kid who was sneaking out unnoticed when he didn't even glance twice at her.

At the corner, she hailed a cab to the Everest Air offices. Her iPhone buzzed, letting her know she had a text message.

She loved the iPhone function that made the text messages into a conversation. This message was from Bebe and was typical of her friend.

Bebe: How was last night?

Amelia: Nice. Will tell you later when we have drinks.

Bebe: No way. I want the story behind that kiss. It looked like it was more than nice.

Amelia realized that she had no idea how to describe what was happening between her and Geoff. She really didn't want to, either. Everything was new and fresh between them and she wanted to keep it to herself for a while.

But the published photo had made that impossible. It was something that she'd never considered before. Living her life in front of the camera had made sense for the young woman she had been, but the woman she was becoming might appreciate some privacy

Amelia: Can't chat now. Let's talk later.

Bebe: Is he with you?

Amelia: Not now. I'm on my way to meet him.

Bebe: TTYL

Amelia resisted typing in text language because she loved words and it made her crazy to see things like *gr8*. She just couldn't make herself use those abbreviations.

The cabbie pulled up in front of the office and she stepped out of the car. As the cab pulled away, she caught a glimpse of herself in the plate-glass doors of Everest Air offices. She thought she looked very nice today, if she did say so herself. She hoped Geoff would think so, too.

She slung her Coach bag over her shoulder and walked

toward the building. The door opened as she approached and a tall, blond man walked out.

"Hello."

She smiled at him. "Hi."

"Can I help you?" he asked.

"I'm here to see Geoff Devonshire."

"Just my luck. I'm Grant, Geoff's second-in-command," he said, holding his hand out to her.

"Amelia Munroe," she said, taking off her glasses and taking his hand.

"You are even prettier in person than you are in your pictures."

"I won't keep you," she said graciously. He had that look in his eyes—the one that made her suspect he'd seen her YouTube video.

"I'll show you up to Geoff's office," Grant offered.

She couldn't think of a polite way to decline so she went into the building. The security guard, however, came to her aid.

"I'll need some ID, please, and to confirm your appointment with Mr. Devonshire."

"She's with me, Will," Grant said to the security guard. "This is Ms. Amelia Munroe."

"There are no exceptions, Grant. You know that."

Grant looked at his watch and then smiled at Amelia. "I'll leave you in Will's hands. It was very nice to meet you."

Grant left and Amelia was relieved to see him go. Being the woman that she was, Grant's reaction was one she was used to. But now that she was trying to keep a low profile for Geoff's sake, it had made her feel a bit odd to have a man staring at her like that.

"I'm not sure if I'm on his calendar yet. We spoke this morning," she said to the guard.

"You are in fact expected. But I need to see your ID and verify that he is in before I send you up."

She nodded and handed him her photo ID, thinking about the conversation she and Geoff were about to have. She had sent a message to Auggie this morning telling him that she was going to explain his absence by saying he was on a research trip to check out some of the newer Munroe Hotels. He had yet to get back to her, but she knew her brother would be more than happy to travel to the latest hotel opening and report back on its success.

She thought that moving him out of the executive offices and into a public role would be the best solution to Auggie's boredom and the board's impatience with him.

Now she just had to figure out how to convince them both that the solution she'd come up with would work. But she was confident she could do it, especially if she and Geoff could work out a partnership deal. The board would be ecstatic at the thought of a joint venture with an Everest company. It was a win-win situation.

"Here you go, Ms. Munroe," Will said, handing back her ID. She tucked it into her wallet while he called Geoff's office. And it was then that she realized she didn't know his numbers—any of them. He knew her address, but that was it.

She'd spent the night with him and she had no idea where he lived or how to get in touch with him. And that was a very weird feeling.

How was she going to ask for his number without appearing clingy?

This was uncharted territory for her and she had absolutely no idea how to react. What was it she was supposed to do?

"You are cleared to go up, Ms. Munroe," Will said. He pushed a button under his desk and the glass door leading into the elevator area buzzed. She walked over to it and opened it.

She went to the elevator, reminding herself that Geoff had suggested this. He wanted to see her. She knew he'd be thrilled that she wanted to pursue the partnership. She just had to relax and enjoy being with him. But in the back of her mind was that fear—that it wouldn't last.

Geoff looked up as Amelia entered his office, stunned by the sight of her in classic clothes. She took his breath away. Maybe it was the fact that he now knew the body underneath the suit. Or maybe it was just that he now knew her better than he had before.

God, he was starting to sound like a sap. What was his problem? She was still just a woman. One who could set him on fire just by entering a room, but still, she was just a woman. A woman who was here to conduct business.

He stood up to greet her. When his secretary left, he was tempted to pull Amelia into his arms and kiss her. But he resisted. He had to start controlling his impulses around her.

"You look lovely," he said. "This isn't your normal type of outfit, is it?"

"No, it isn't. I decided to try this out because we are doing business together and…the paparazzi aren't used to seeing me this way. I walked right past one of them who is always hanging out at my front door. He didn't even recognize me."

"That *is* good," he said, unable to keep his eyes from roaming over her body. "Please, have a seat. Can I get you a coffee or some water?"

"Water would be great," she said.

He pulled bottles of Evian from the refrigerator in his credenza and poured them both into highball glasses. Then he leaned back against his desk, not wanting to be too far away from her.

"Have you made a decision?" he asked her.

"I have. I'd like to proceed," she said, sounding strangely formal and slightly nervous.

"Wonderful. I've had a chance to talk to one of my managers about packaging our brands and he thinks it's a great idea. He'll be working with us on the project."

"Who is it?"

"Carson Miller. Why?"

"I met Grant downstairs and he seemed very familiar with me, did you mention the deal to him?" she asked.

Geoff caught a flash of something in her eyes and he wondered if Grant had tried to flirt with her.

"Did he make you uncomfortable?" he asked her.

She shrugged and tipped her head to the side. "Not really, but he was a little too friendly. And I'd rather not work with him."

"I'll speak with him," Geoff said.

She shook her head. "Don't do that. It was just me being silly."

"Silly in what way?" he asked.

She put her water glass down and stood up, walking over to his window with a view of Heathrow Airport.

"You made me realize last night that I am more than videos and publicity stunts, and he reminded me that to the rest of the world, I'm not."

Geoff didn't know how to respond to that. To him Amelia was always more than a girl in a video. And to most people she met she would always be. Because of the charity work she'd done and just her personality, she projected more than someone in a scandalous video would. But to a certain kind of man she'd never be more than her public persona.

"Amelia, if I talk to him—"

She turned around. "No, you shouldn't. That would just make matters worse. Tell me about Carson, and what you will need from Munroe Hotels."

He walked around behind his desk and sat down. "Give me your e-mail address and I'll forward the information to you."

"It's amunroe@munroehotels.com," she said. "I realized earlier I don't have any of your numbers."

"Nor I yours," he said, pulling out his iPhone and smiling at her. "Why don't you give them to me now?"

A second later they'd exchanged information. "Are you available this weekend?"

"For?"

"A trip to Bath. I have a house there and I thought it'd be nice to spend the weekend away from the city together."

She chewed her lower lip as she mulled over his invitation. "I'd like that."

"Good. My mother wants to meet you so I thought I'd invite her to dinner on Saturday."

"Your mother? Geoff, I'm not sure about that," she said.

Geoff wasn't a man who was used to hearing the word *no*. And he certainly wasn't going to let Amelia decline. "I promise, it will not be painful at all. She's a nice lady and she asked about you specifically."

"Does she want to talk to me about the photo in *The Sun?*"

Geoff had the feeling he was going to be on trial more than Amelia. His mother had always been very sensitive to the women he dated, always making sure he treated them properly. As if he wouldn't. He was her son and he certainly understood that women could be badly hurt by a callous man.

"I think she wants to meet you because we are dating."

Her eyes widened. "Are we dating?"

"I told you I want to let things develop."

"So that means we are dating in your mind. You should have said something."

"I just did," he said, grinning at her.

She shook her head. "You are one bossy man."

"Is that a problem?" he asked enjoying sparring with her. He could tell she was enjoying herself, too, by the sparkle in her eyes.

"I haven't decided yet."

He stood and walked around his desk. "Let me know when you do."

He put his hands on her narrow waist and drew her closer to him. She tilted her head back, anticipating his kiss.

He toyed with her for a moment before bringing his

mouth down on hers with the pent-up passion of having been in her presence without touching her. He knew that this business deal was going to be complicated because keeping his mind off her and on the bottom line was more difficult than he'd expected.

Amelia felt confused as Geoff kissed her. He had been so cool and businesslike when she'd first entered his office but now he was the passionate man she'd spent the night with. A knock on his door had him pulling away and again, she wasn't sure how to act.

Then she realized that she was being ridiculous. She couldn't let one man shake her so much. She tossed her head as the door opened.

"I'm sorry to interrupt, but Carson is here with some numbers for you. He said he thought you needed them for this meeting," his secretary said.

"We do. Please send him in," Geoff said. "Do you have time for a quick rundown of the proposal Carson has put together?"

Amelia pulled out her cell phone and glanced at her schedule. The only way she'd make her luncheon was if she left immediately from here. And that wouldn't work because she'd wanted to go home and change back into her normal clothes. "I can spare maybe five minutes. I have a luncheon at one and I need time to go home and change."

His brow creased and as the door opened he turned to the man and said, "Give me a moment." Geoff closed the door and leaned back against it. "Why do you need to change?"

"If I go to the luncheon dressed like this, then

everyone will know that I've changed. This luncheon is for teenaged mothers…I am going to use every media connection I have to bring attention to their need. I can't risk our relationship—"

She stopped as she realized what she was saying. Her motivation was her desire to keep her relationship with Geoff quiet—because he had asked her to. For a second, she worried that he was ashamed of her, and that was why he wanted to keep things quiet.

"Thank you, Amelia. I didn't realize how complicated this was going to be."

She had. "It's not a big deal but I will be later than is acceptable if I don't head out soon. Why don't you just e-mail me the figures Carson came up with? Do you suppose your secretary will call a cab for me?"

"She will. When can you meet again to discuss the details of our joint venture?" he asked.

She glanced down at her schedule again. "I can do it on Thursday, or early next week. I'm going to talk to my marketing person at Munroe this afternoon and I'll forward to her the e-mail you send me from Carson. Will that work?"

"Yes. I think next week is a good time to meet," he said. "But of course I'll be seeing you before then."

"Will you pick me up on Friday night or do you want me to meet you in Bath?"

"We can talk about that tonight."

Tonight? Had she missed something? She had accepted a dinner invitation from Lady Abercrombie and she couldn't miss another of her mom's friend's dinner parties. "I have an engagement tonight."

"Break it."

"Geoff! I can't just—"

"I want to take you flying," he said. "I had planned on doing it last night, but desire got the better of me and we ended up in your garden instead." He stared at her with such intensity that her pulse raced.

Flying sounded infinitely more appealing than Cecelia's would ever be. But if she went with him… he'd begin to know that she wanted to be with him all the time.

"You are tempting me," she said.

"Good," he said.

He stood there, just waiting for her answer. And suddenly she had a moment's panic. Was he using her? Was he wining and dining her—and sleeping with her—just to gain access to her family's business? Was she being stupidly naive?

She chewed her lower lip, wanting some kind of sign from him that he wanted to spend more time with her because he had real feelings, not because he was trying to manipulate her into a deal.

"What are you thinking?" he asked.

She thought long and hard before she answered. Was she going to treat Geoff the way she treated all the men she dated, or should she be honest and bare her soul, letting him see all her imperfections and insecurities?

What if he didn't like her? she thought. She'd never been good enough for any man before. Not the woman she was in front of the flashbulbs and the media attention, and with Geoff she wanted to be.

"Amelia?"

"I'm scared," she admitted.

"Of me?" he asked.

She shook her head. "Of letting you see the real me and finding out that you don't like her at all."

Geoff reached for her hand. "I adore you, Amelia. How could I not like a single thing about you?"

"Plenty of people don't."

"I am not 'plenty of people.' I know you in a different way, in a real way," he said. "This is all new territory for me, too. I'm trying to figure out how to make this into a relationship, but I've never been involved with a woman like you before."

"Okay," she said, looking into his eyes. "I'll go flying with you tonight. Should I meet you at the airport?"

"Why don't you do that? I keep my plane at London City Airport."

He gave her further details and she started to leave. But something pulled her back and pushed her right into his arms.

She gave him a kiss designed to arouse him and then stepped away. "So that you won't forget me this afternoon."

"It isn't possible, love, believe me," he said, his voice husky.

She winked at him and walked out the door.

Eight

Geoff walked into the Athenaeum Club as though he owned it. No matter what Edmond thought, there was little he or Malcolm could do to make him change his mind about Amelia. Geoff's place in society had been cemented by years of clean living and duty. He was meeting his half brothers for drinks, something the other fellows wanted to make a ritual.

And since the novelty of actually talking to the other Devonshire bastards hadn't worn off, he didn't mind meeting them.

He took a seat in the back of the bar and waited for Henry and Steven to arrive. Steven's idea to have all of their mothers interviewed in *Fashion Quarterly* was proving to be a pain. He understood that they wanted to generate buzz around the new Everest Group but Geoff was highly private. Letting anyone in was anathema.

Though now that he was dating Amelia Munroe he might have to revise that.

"Hello, mate!" Henry said as he approached the table.

Geoff stood and shook his hand. "Good afternoon."

"Seen a bit of you in the papers," Henry said.

"Just a bit," Geoff replied, shaking his head. "It will die down."

"You better hope it does. Edmond is a stickler about that scandal clause in the will," Steven said as he joined them.

"There is nothing scandalous about my relationship with Amelia."

"What is your relationship?" Steven asked.

"None of your business," Geoff responded.

Henry leaned forward. "I get that, mate, but if you are going to be in the papers…"

Geoff didn't like having to explain himself to anyone, especially these two. He was the oldest of them and he should be the one they deferred to. "Not that it matters, but we are talking about a business deal between the airline and Munroe Hotels."

Steven nodded. "Great idea. I think that's enough to keep Edmond off your back."

"How do you know about Edmond?" Geoff asked.

"He's calling all of us…trying to make sure we're not following in dear old Dad's footsteps, I'm sure," Henry said.

Steven laughed and Geoff shook his head. "We don't even know the man, how could we be anything like him?"

"Beats me. I'm just glad to know that I'm not the only one getting calls," Steven said.

"Me, too," Geoff added.

The men settled back to drink their drinks and discuss the business of the Everest Group, and for the first time since Edmond had called this afternoon, Geoff felt a sense of peace about the entire deal with Amelia. He knew how to manage his personal life and how to make sure that she knew where she stood in it.

Amelia dressed carefully for her evening with Geoff, putting on a pair of slim-fitting jeans and a designer top. She wrapped a scarf around her neck and then donned a leather bomber-style jacket. She put her hair up in a high ponytail as she checked her look in the mirror one more time.

Her afternoon had been full and busy, but she'd discovered that having Geoff's contact information was interesting. She kept wondering what he was doing and had been tempted to call him at least six times, but she'd resisted.

Everything about him made her feel unsure and excited at the same time. She wanted to know where he was and if he was thinking about her, but at the same time was so afraid to ask him and she hated the fear.

She'd always known exactly who she was and what she wanted from life. And now Geoff Devonshire was making her question all of it. Because now she wished to be the kind of woman that he wanted her to be.

She had tried to be one man's ideal before and it hadn't worked out for her. In fact, she was often trying to fill a need in a man, she thought. With her father, it had been dutiful daughter. With her brother, it was responsible sister. With other men, it had been exotic, sexy girlfriend. And all those roles had left her wanting.

She was all of those things and so much more and she was just beginning to understand that she needed to let herself be who she really was.

Her cell phone rang and she was tempted to let it go to voice mail but she needed a distraction from her own thoughts.

"This is Amelia," she said.

"It's Auggie. I got your message," he said. She heard music playing in the background and knew he was either in his car or at his place.

"What do you think? The board is adamant. They want to see something new from you or you're out," she said.

"And you're in? Is that what your agenda is?" Auggie asked.

He sounded paranoid, which probably meant one thing—he was using drugs. She closed her eyes, not ready to deal with her brother the addict again. "You know I'm not trying to take over your position. I'm trying to help you."

"Are you, Lia? I'm not sure anymore. Vickers told me that you argued with the board for a change in roles for me," he said.

"I did make that point but only because you hate being in the office. I've been thinking that you should be the new face of Munroe Hotels."

"You think so?"

"Yes. People want to stay with someone they know. I'm also working on a joint promotion with Everest Air that I think will bring in extra revenue. What do you think? You know the board better than I do, but I want to give them more profit to think about, instead of your absences from the executive offices."

"I like it, Lia. I'm sorry I thought you were out to get me," he said, sounding like his old self.

"No problem," she replied. She was never going to tell him about the fear that gripped her whenever she thought about him using again. Auggie hadn't handled the lifestyle as well as some of his peers. While she'd turned to scandalous behavior to deal with the pressure, Auggie had turned to drugs and it had almost ruined his life.

"Love you, sis."

"Love you, too," she said, hanging up. As much of a pain in the neck as he was, she needed her brother. She needed to know that he was going to be calling her and asking her to take care of things for him. He was a man that she knew how to deal with, she thought.

Maybe she hadn't always disappointed the men in her life. And with Auggie, she was her true self. She didn't have to pretend to be someone other than who she was. He had known her since birth.

Interesting, she thought. Maybe there was more to being herself than she'd realized. Maybe this was the key to the balance she craved.

She put on a final dash of lip gloss and headed out the door. She'd planned on driving herself, but the rain had changed her mind. She'd never really liked to drive in inclement weather.

If she took her car, Tommy and the other paparazzi would know where she was going and who she was meeting. She sat down on the edge of her bed. This was harder than it should be.

She'd changed clothes more times than she normally would today. She'd been sneaking in and out of her own apartment building and now she was going to have to… what?

Bebe. She'd call her friend. Surely Bebe could help her out.

She dialed Bebe's number.

"Hello, darling," Bebe said.

"I need a favor."

"Okay, what do you need?"

"I have a date with Geoff tonight and I don't want anyone to follow me. How would you feel about coming over here and providing some distraction?"

"I'd love to, but your boys aren't going to follow me," Bebe said.

"I know. I was thinking we could go together to a club and then I could sneak out the back."

"Why don't you just drive?"

"It's very wet tonight and my car is so recognizable," Amelia said. She had a vividly painted Jaguar that was very memorable, which was why she'd bought it. She liked people knowing she was behind the wheel, but not tonight.

Bebe laughed. "Come to my place. My dad's here and he can drive you wherever you're going."

"Your dad?"

"He has the Rolls and you know that you'd never be seen in a stodgy car like that unless you were going to visit your own father. They aren't likely to follow you in that car."

Bebe had a point. Amelia hung up and was on her way to Bebe's house a few minutes later in a cab. And though she knew she should be annoyed at all the subterfuge she was going through, she wasn't. She was simply excited at the prospect of seeing Geoff again.

Geoff was running behind schedule—something that rarely happened to him. He was driving his Bugatti Veyron toward London City Airport when his mobile phone rang.

"Devonshire."

"Hi, Geoff. It's Mary. Mary Werner."

"Hello, Mary. Can I give you a ring tomorrow? I can't really talk right now."

"That's fine. I just…well, I saw your photo in *The Sun* today and I wondered if you were still going to the breast cancer dinner with me next week."

He hadn't even thought to call Mary when the photo had appeared, which was not his classiest move. He realized that he needed to end things with her officially, even though she clearly already knew what the story was. "I think I can still manage that if you'd like me to."

"I would, Geoff. It would mean a lot to me, even though you are…uh…" She trailed off, unable to finish her sentence.

"I'm sorry, Mary. I should have called you. I know that we'd been dating a lot but—"

"Say no more, Geoff. I wasn't expecting an offer for my hand. We are really more friends than lovers, aren't we?"

"Yes, I think we are." Geoff couldn't tell if she was

upset or relieved. But she was a lot like him and he knew that duty came first to her. "I'm sorry things weren't different between us."

"Me, too. I like you but I think we would have bored each other to tears," she said.

He laughed. "We are similar."

"And you certainly never kissed me like you kissed Amelia."

"I think you'll find a man who will kiss you like that," he said.

"I'm going to. When I saw that photo this morning I was hurt, of course, but more than that I was envious. I want a man to kiss me that way and not care that the entire world is watching."

"I hope you find him," Geoff said. He wanted her to be happy.

"I'll see you next Wednesday?"

"Yes. I'll pick you up."

"Good night, Geoff."

Geoff felt relief that things had ended between him and Mary. They would have made a fine couple because they were both people who honored their commitments, but life would have been a quiet, slow death, he thought.

Having been with Amelia now, he knew he couldn't marry for his family's sake anymore. He needed a woman who stirred his passion. He needed a woman who painted his world with color, not bland responsibility. He needed Amelia.

His mobile phone rang again and he answered it.

"It's Henry."

"What can I do for you, Henry?" Geoff asked. Despite

the drinks they'd had at his club the other night he hardly knew his half brother.

"I wanted to invite you to a London-Irish game. My stepfather is the coach."

"I'd like that. When is it?" Geoff asked. He got the details from Henry. As Henry spoke, he decided to ask him for a word of advice.

"You have the media following you around a lot. How do you deal with it?" Geoff finally asked.

"I pretend that they aren't there. They are going to follow me anyway, and I can't deal with them so I ignore them. Why? Does this have anything to do with Amelia Munroe?"

Geoff wondered if he should have kept his mouth shut, but he wanted someone else's opinion and Henry was the only man he knew in this kind of situation.

"Yes, it does."

"I don't get the kind of coverage that she does. They follow her everywhere. But I find that just living your life is best. If you start trying to avoid them it can be a headache, and they always find you no matter what you do."

"That's not what I was hoping to hear."

"What did you want—a way to get rid of them completely?"

"Maybe."

Henry laughed, a jovial sound that made Geoff smile. "That's not going to happen, mate. *Ever.* Even if you weren't dating Amelia, they would still follow you because of Malcolm."

"They usually leave me be on that account," he said. Probably because of his mum. When the rumors circulated that she'd been put in the hospital for psychiatric evaluation and his stepfather had moved them out to the country for several years, the press actually took a step back.

"Have you talked to that Ainsley Patterson at British *Fashion Quarterly* about the interviews she wants to do? My mum is over the moon. She'd love to have her face in a magazine."

"She has a very lovely face," Geoff said. "My mum's not so keen on being in the article."

"I figured as much. I'm not sure that talking about the past is the right way to go. My family is used to the spotlight, though."

"That is true. What did Steven's mum say?"

"I heard he was going to Berne to talk to her in person. Steven believes this kind of article will help investors feel that the Everest Group is secure and that they won't need to worry about the future once Malcolm kicks it."

"Kicks it?"

"You know what I mean," Henry said.

"Steven has a lot of ideas about the company and they are usually solid. Edmond is very meddlesome when it comes to running our businesses," Geoff said.

"He is, and he's not afraid to butt into your personal business, either," Henry said.

"Indeed."

"I saw the photo of you and Amelia in *The Sun.* I don't think there is anything to worry about, but Edmond is of a different generation. He saw Malcolm almost lose the entire Everest Group when the situation with our mums went public. He'll do whatever he has to make sure that the company stays solvent."

"I don't answer to him," Geoff said.

"I hear you," Henry replied. "Your life is your own. Just watch your back—Edmond's not going to let you, Steven or me mess up the Everest Group."

"Thanks. How's the record label?"

"Good. I never thought I'd like it as much as I do," Henry said.

They chatted a few more minutes before he arrived at the hangar where his plane was kept and he hung up with Henry. He thought about what his half brother had said about Edmond, and Geoff knew he'd have to work the older man carefully because he wasn't about to give up Amelia.

Bebe's parents were at her house for their weekly dinner. Amelia had always envied her friend's close relationship with her family. Carlotta and Davis were both in their late fifties, and were a very attractive, romantic couple. They still held hands when they were in the same room, and she and Bebe had on more than one occasion walked in on them smooching.

"Do you have time for a drink?" Bebe asked.

"I'd love one," she said.

"Good. Dad's just mixed a pitcher of martinis. And they are pure perfection."

Bebe poured her a cocktail and then sat down next to her on the love seat in the sitting room. The walls were decorated in a soft blue with creamy white accents.

"Tell me about your date last night. And then I want

to know what he has planned for tonight," Bebe said. "This is exciting."

"Exciting?"

"Because you've never dated a man like Geoff Devonshire before."

"Geoff Devonshire," Carlotta said. "Is that who you're going out with? He's not your usual sort of man, is he?"

"Mom, not now. I want to get the details first."

"I know his mom, Amelia," Carlotta said.

Suddenly Amelia had a chance to learn everything she wanted to know about Geoff and his family. An unexpected feeling of relief washed over her. "I think I might meet her this weekend."

"Then it must be serious," Carlotta said. "He isn't the kind of man to bring home the women he dates."

"We've only been out once," she said, not wanting them to read anything into a relationship that she wasn't sure would last.

"And they are going out again tonight," Bebe said.

"And he already wants you to meet Louisa? That's encouraging. When Davis was courting me, I wanted to spend every second with him. When we were apart, I missed him desperately."

"That was, like, thirty years ago, Mom," Bebe said.

"But love doesn't change," Carlotta said.

"I don't know that this is love. We've only had one date."

Carlotta nodded. "But it feels different, right?"

"What feels different?" Amelia asked.

"Being with him. Don't you find that he's different from all the other men you've dated?"

"He's very different," she admitted. And that was part of why she was so enamored of him. But love? She wasn't ready to accept that. It was too soon. Everything was happening too fast.

She took another sip of her martini and realized that coming here and talking like this—about love—was making her nervous. What if Geoff couldn't love her?

Did that matter? Did she want him to fall in love with her? She had never dreamed of marriage because her own parents had made such a mess of it. But every once in a while, she'd thought that it would be nice to have a relationship like Bebe's parents had.

"I'm sure you two will make a good match. What time do you need to leave? Davis is ready to play chauffeur for you."

"Thank you, Carlotta. I'm ready to go now," Amelia said.

"Not so fast. I haven't heard any of the juicy details," Bebe said.

"I'll leave so she can tell you," Carlotta said. She patted Amelia on the shoulder as she went by, then stopped and looked back. "Being in love is the most wonderful feeling, Amelia, but it can also be very scary. It sometimes feels as if you're losing yourself."

Carlotta left and Bebe scooted closer to Amelia on the love seat, wrapping her arm around Amelia's shoulders. "Does it feel that way?"

"I don't know. I don't know what to do. A part of me wants him to love me and would do anything to make that happen. I mean, look at me, I'm sneaking around and changing cars like a spy in a James Bond movie."

"And the other part?" Bebe asked.

She shrugged. How could she put it into words? She felt just the way Carlotta had described—scared and euphoric at the same time.

"I just don't know. I've never felt this way about a man before."

"I think that's a good thing, darling. Let's decide that it is."

"And deciding will make it so?"

"Yes, it will. If things get serious I get to be your maid of honor," Bebe said.

Amelia shook her head. "Don't even talk about marriage. I'm not sure I can handle falling in love. What if I do but he doesn't? Or what if he wants me to change even more? He already has me trying to avoid photographers, which I've never done."

Bebe hugged her close. "You wouldn't do any of that unless you wanted to. This man isn't changing you, he's allowing you to be different. That's not a bad thing."

Amelia wasn't too sure about that. "I hope so."

"Darling, you know that you haven't been the scandalous heiress in years. The most daring thing you've done is jog around Hyde Park in a skimpy running outfit."

"True. I have changed. With Geoff, I'm going to have to give up the last part of that heiress I used to be."

"Used to be," Bebe said. "Don't be afraid to be the new you."

She'd never liked the old her and she wasn't sure who the "new" Amelia would be. But being with Geoff felt right, and as Davis dropped her off at the hangar, she didn't feel like this was a second date. She felt like this was the start of her new life.

Nine

Geoff had brought a picnic dinner and set it up in the hangar. When Amelia walked in, he felt a rush of emotion he couldn't identify and didn't even try. He had never met anyone who affected him as strongly as she did. She looked sexy and unsure as she paused in the doorway—it took every ounce of willpower he had not to go to her.

She glanced at the blanket he'd spread out on the floor. "We're having a picnic."

"I hope that's okay," he said.

"It's...perfect. Thank you," she said, her eyes lighting up as she took in the blanket, the food and the roses.

"How did you get here?" he asked, wondering if their picnic would be interrupted by paparazzi. He wanted privacy and the chance to enjoy himself with this beautiful woman he was coming to care deeply about.

But by the same token he didn't want her to have to jump through hoops to see him.

"Bebe's father drove me after the paparazzi left, figuring I was spending the night there. I was going to drive myself but everyone knows my car. And I don't like to drive in the rain."

"Why not?"

"I had an accident. I was fine but it shook me up. I hit another car when mine hydroplaned. It made me realize I couldn't control anything."

"How old were you?"

"Twenty-five. It's funny because, at the time, my life was kind of spiraling out of control. That was right about the time that the video hit YouTube and I was just acting out a lot. Wearing outrageous clothing and making sure that everything printed about me was titillating. And then the car accident happened," she said.

"But you were okay?"

"I was. I was taken to the hospital because of a scrape on my forehead. I had a concussion and the papers said I'd been drinking, of course."

"Had you been?" he asked.

"No. And I learned the hard way that the media just made up what they wanted to in order to sell more papers. I disappeared for a few weeks and came back with an agenda. Then I started really working for the Munroe Foundation. That accident changed my life," she said.

"I'm glad," he said. "And very happy you were okay."

He pulled her into his arms and hugged her close. Though she'd talked about the accident like it was no big deal, he realized that he might never have met her if things had seriously gone wrong. What would it be like if he didn't have Amelia? What if something took her away from him?

His thoughts turned to his phone call with Edmond. He had planned to tell her about it tonight, but he decided that business could wait. They could put out all the fires tomorrow. Tonight was about them.

She wrapped her arms around his waist and rested her head against his chest right over his heart. And though the self-protective part of him wanted to believe that this was just about lust and obsession, he knew deep inside that there was something more at work here.

He stepped back from her and led the way to the picnic he'd laid out.

"I hope you like chicken marsala."

"Love it. My mom's Italian, as you know."

"Can she cook?" he asked, pulling her down next to him on the blanket.

Amelia laughed. "Yes, but she doesn't. She has a chef. Though to be honest, she never did much cooking, even before she was 'Mia Domenici, famous fashion designer'."

"Wasn't she always famous?" Geoff asked.

"She was a model first. She started designing when my brother and I were toddlers. She attributes her success to being home with us."

"That's nice. She made you a part of her business then."

Amelia smiled. "I'd never thought of it that way before. I always thought she was bored with us."

"Or she didn't want to just be a stay-at-home mum.

Maybe she wanted you both to have something else to aspire to," Geoff said. He handed her a plate, sat down next to her and uncorked the wine.

"And look how that worked out. We both spend most of our time jet-setting around the world."

"And working for your father's company," he added. "I think you sell yourself short."

"It's easier to do that than to have someone else tell you that you don't measure up."

"You measure up very nicely, Amelia," he said.

He handed her a glass of wine and lifted his own for a toast.

"Salut!" she said.

"Salut."

They both took a sip. "What kind of car is that?" she asked, eyeing the sports car he'd parked in the hangar.

"A Veyron," he said. "They're very fast."

"They're also very hard to come by. You have to wait for them to be made, right?"

"Yes. But I put my name on the list a long time ago so when they started producing this model, I got one of the first ones."

"Why do you want a car like that?" she asked.

"I like to go fast. I've always had a thing for cars and planes."

"Let me guess. Probably because when you're at the controls of a plane or behind the wheel of a car, no one knows who you are," she said.

"Exactly," he said. "Driving is the closest I get on the ground to the feeling flying brings me."

"Truly?" she asked. "Just driving?"

"Well, until recently. I've found something else that makes me feel like I'm flying."

"What is that?" she asked.

"You," he said.

She looked up at him with those wide blue eyes of hers and he felt his heart skip a beat. "Me?"

He nodded.

She bit her lower lip and he reached across the blanket to stroke the side of her face. "What is it?"

"I just realized that I'm afraid to believe you."

"Don't be," he said.

"What if I fall?" she asked.

"I'll catch you," he said. And those words were more than reassurance, they were a promise that he knew he never wanted to break.

Amelia had never been in the cockpit of a plane before. She liked watching Geoff ready the small aircraft for takeoff. He showed her what he was doing as he did it, including her in every aspect of the preparations. She sat next to him as they taxied down the runway once they were given the all clear, and then they were in the air.

The cloud cover that had produced the rain earlier was gone and it was a clear night. They had headphones on so they could speak to each other, and Geoff gave her an aerial tour of the city, pointing out different neighborhoods and landmarks.

Some of it she could easily identify, but other parts were a mystery to her, as if she were seeing London for the first time. In the air, she heard the excitement in Geoff's voice. She could easily see why he'd had a successful career in the RAF. He was made to fly.

"I love this," she said. "I've never seen London like this."

"Up here you can see the entire city from a new perspective."

"It's beautiful at night. I've always liked the nighttime the best," she said.

"Why?"

She shrugged. "I think because at night, no one expects anything from you."

He laughed. "It's okay to mess up at night, is that what you're saying?"

"Yes, it is. Think about it. During the day, everyone has claims on you. But at night no one has any designs on what you should be doing. They might wish you were at home or perhaps doing something respectable, but no one expects you to be working."

"I think you're right to some extent. There are still obligations at night but you can beg off and the host won't think less of you," Geoff said.

Amelia knew that while she saw the evenings as a time to play and relax, Geoff and polite society saw things differently. For them, it was a time to shine.

"How did you get out of your dinner tonight?" he asked.

"By promising to have brunch with Cecelia in two weeks' time," she said. "She really is a dear friend of Mom's so I felt bad canceling. But she suspected that I might be canceling to spend time with you, so she was okay with that."

"She was? Why?"

Amelia got uncomfortable. Why had she brought this up? Everyone thought that Geoff was different from the usual men she dated. People like Cecelia and Carlotta thought that meant that she might settle down. But Amelia worried that she was Geoff's last wild fling before he found himself a respectable wife like Mary Werner—a woman who would never make waves and always say and do the right thing.

"She thinks you're a nice man."

"Nice?"

"Yes. That's a good thing, you know."

"It sounds boring. No man wants to be boring, especially when he's with you."

"I don't think you are boring," she said. "How could I?"

"Good. Now, do you want to take the controls?"

She shook her head. "No way. I like watching you do your thing."

"But I can't touch you if I'm flying," he said.

His words sent a pulse of desire straight through her body, making her moist at her center. She wanted his hands on her again. It felt like ages since last night.

"I definitely don't want to be in control of the airplane if you're going to touch me. I'd probably make us crash."

"Do I have the power to do that?"

"Yes, you do," she said. She took a deep breath. "You have more power over me than any other man ever has."

"And how does that make you feel?" he asked.

"Scared," she said. "Because I have no idea how you feel."

He banked the plane and started heading back toward the city. "You make me feel alive, Amelia. In a way that nothing has before—not even my fast cars and jet planes."

Amelia wrapped an arm around her waist and hugged herself. This was more than she'd expected him to admit. Was Geoff falling for her? She wanted to believe that.

Almost too much. Was she making Geoff into the hero that she'd always been afraid to hope would show up?

She reached over and put her hand on his leg as he continued piloting the plane. She loved the feel of his muscular thigh.

"I like it when you touch me," he said.

"I like touching you. I can't get enough of you."

"Really?"

"Can't you tell? Last night I told myself that I'd only have one night with you. But here I am again."

"What changed your mind?" he asked.

"You did," she admitted. "This morning, when you stood naked in my kitchen."

"Hmm…you can't resist a naked man?" he asked.

She looked over at Geoff and smiled. He knew that it was much more than not being able to resist a naked man—it was that she couldn't resist a naked Geoff. She could see that he knew he was the part that changed the equation. She wanted to build dreams around him—and that was dangerous.

Geoff landed the plane and pulled into the hangar but made no move to get out. He took his headphones off and helped Amelia with hers.

"Thank you for taking me flying," she said. "I've never done anything like that before. It was spectacular."

"I'm glad you liked it," he said. He'd really enjoyed having her with him in the plane. "I have a biplane with an open cockpit that I'll take you up in sometime. You'll really like that."

"Why?"

"Because you can feel the wind in your hair. I'll do a couple of barrel rolls so you can get the full effect."

"Full effect of what? Watching my life flash in front of my eyes?" she asked.

"You wouldn't be in any danger. It's exhilarating."

"You might think so, Mr. Daredevil, but I think I'll stick to a nice evening flight in a contained cockpit."

"As long as you're in my cockpit, I'm okay with that," he said.

She looked gorgeous, sitting in his plane. He'd been rock hard since she put her hand on his thigh, and now that they were back on the ground, he wanted her naked.

He reached over and slowly unwound the scarf from her neck, leaving the ends hanging down her body. "Take off your jacket."

She looked up at him and arched one eyebrow. "Am I finally going to feel your hands on me?"

"Oh, yes," he said.

"It's about time," she said with a cheeky grin.

"I want your breasts, Amelia. Take off your jacket and your blouse, but leave on that scarf."

A light flush covered her skin as she did what he asked. He watched as every inch of her torso was revealed to him. When she was naked from the waist up, he reached over to touch her left nipple. He'd noticed last night that her breasts were very sensitive and he wanted to play with them again, to get her as turned on as he was.

He rubbed his finger lightly over her nipple and then took the scarf and drew it over the tip. She shivered a little and bit her lower lip.

"Do you like that?"

"Very much."

He took the other side of the scarf and rubbed her right breast with it. Then he lightly pulled the scarf back and forth, teasing her breasts into taut peaks.

She squirmed in her seat and then leaned over and pulled his head to hers. His mouth met hers and she devoured him, her tongue thrusting deep into his mouth and her hands clutching at his shoulders. He moved the scarf back and forth faster and felt her fingers tighten on him.

"I want you, Geoff."

"Not yet," he said. "I want to see if you can come from this."

"No," she said. "I want to come with you inside me. Get naked."

He smiled at her sexual demands. She shifted her hips on the seat until she could push her skinny jeans and panties down her legs. And her crotch was offered up to him. He stopped thinking of anything but touching her and tasting her.

He reached over, tracing the thin line of hair on the center of her feminine mound. She was waxed smooth everywhere else. He leaned in closer and pressed his mouth to her, kissed her lightly and breathed in the feminine scent of her secrets.

"Geoff, what are you doing?" she gasped.

"Tasting you," he said.

He parted her with his fingers and ran his tongue down the center of her body, tickling the bud of pleasure revealed there. Her legs shifted to let him closer and he felt her hands in his hair.

He reached up and tweaked one nipple, and heard her gasp again. With his other hand he found the entrance of her body and thrust one finger up inside of her.

She arched her back and moaned loudly. He knew she was about to come and couldn't resist driving her over the edge. He used his mouth and hands to make her crazy until she was calling his name. He felt her core tightening around his fingers.

She leaned limply against the seat and reached down to unzip his pants. He quickly pushed them down over his hips along with his underwear and drew her over the console to straddle him.

She shifted on his lap, reaching down to position him at the center of her body. Then she impaled herself on him. She pulled his mouth to hers and he kissed her briefly, wanting to taste her breasts. He leaned down and took her nipple into his mouth, licking and sucking her.

He pulled strongly on her breasts with his mouth as she moved up and down on his erection. He loved the way she felt wrapped around him. He couldn't get enough of her.

She moaned his name and clutched at his shoulders.

He put his hands on her hips to hurry her movements as he felt his orgasm building.

He was about to spill himself into her but he wanted to make sure she came again. He bit down on her sensitive nipples to push her to the brink.

She tightened and called his name just as stars exploded behind his eyes. He groaned loudly and rocked up into her body three more times before he felt drained.

He rested his head against her breast and held her tightly to him as they both caught their breath.

Here in her arms he didn't think about the fact that they might be too different to make this work. He didn't think about the fact that obsessions could burn out and leave behind nothing. He didn't think about anything but the way she felt in his arms. And how each breath he took was filled with her.

He knew that he should address the attitude of Edmond and others who thought Amelia Munroe wasn't good enough to run a business or associate with him.

Ten

Geoff's sisters were waiting for him when he came home from work on Friday. He was exhausted. After two days of having the paparazzi follow him around, he was getting seriously tired of the spotlight that Amelia lived in—nothing was going to make him comfortable with it. He had to find some way to escape from the constant attention.

He'd been dodging calls from Edmond and his mother all day long. And now to find Gemma and Caroline here—he was tempted to get in the Veyron and drive away, away from the city and away from everything.

But he'd never been a running away kind of man and he wasn't about to start now.

"Hello, brats."

"Hello, hypocrite," Caro said.

"Is this about Amelia?" he asked.

"Yes. Why is it you can date someone and have your picture in the papers every day but I'm not welcome to bring Paul to your place on Sunday?"

He rubbed his hands through his hair and took a deep breath. "Bring him if you want to. I would enjoy talking to him."

"You have to be nice, Geoff, or I'm going to grill Amelia."

"Go ahead. She can handle herself. Can you say the same for Paul?"

She smiled at him. "Yes, I can. He is a professional."

"Enough, Caro. Geoff, I want to talk to you about Mum," Gemma said.

The older of his two sisters had always been the more serious of the girls. And she also had taken the role of mother hen at a fairly young age.

"Is she okay?"

"I'm not sure. She called me last night to discuss how you are with women," Gemma said. "I think the coverage of you and Amelia is reminding her a little of her relationship with your father."

Geoff didn't like that. The relationship of his mother and his biological father had set his mother on the path to seclusion from the world. It was only when she'd met and married the girls' father that she'd started to come out of her shell again.

"I think meeting Amelia this weekend will help ease her mind. I'm not Malcolm and I'm not toying with Amelia," he said.

"Good," Gemma said. "Now that that is settled. Who should I bring this weekend?"

"Who is on the list?" Caro said.

"You don't have to bring a date," Geoff said. He hadn't been planning on having a huge party—just his mother and sisters and Amelia.

"Well, if Caro is bringing Paul, I should have someone," Gemma said.

"Do you want me to invite someone for you?" he asked. He had already started going through the list of men he thought would be suitable for Gemma to date.

"No. I'll find someone. What time should we be at your place on Sunday?"

"Around noon," he said.

The girls left and Geoff went into his study. He had never thought of himself as Malcolm Devonshire's son, but he knew he resembled his father—more than the other two sons did. They all had Malcolm's eyes but Geoff had his features, too.

For the first time he thought about how that may have affected his mother. She'd always loved him, but seeing him as a grown man must be hard for her. And now, with the media glare on his relationship with Amelia, it seemed to be sending her into a panic.

It became doubly important to him to keep the hounds at bay. Not only so that he could have Amelia to himself but also so that his mother didn't have to relive what had been such a hard time in her life.

His phone rang and he answered it on the second ring.

"Devonshire," he said.

"Geoff, this is Edmond. We need to meet."

"I can probably squeeze you in on Monday, but you'll have to speak to my secretary."

"This can't wait."

"I can't see you this afternoon," Geoff said.

"I'm not going to be put off," Edmond said.

The last thing Geoff wanted was to meet with Edmond this weekend to discuss the older man's views on Amelia. They'd done their best to avoid the media and Everest Air was showing a profit.

"Does this have anything to do with the airline?"

"No, it's about Amelia Munroe. I have already warned you about continuing to see her."

"I'm a grown man, Edmond, you can't tell me what to do. Since the airline is performing better than expected, I don't see what you have to complain about."

Edmond let out a long breath. "Very well. I need to see you this weekend. I have some papers for you to sign."

"What papers?" Geoff asked.

"Your father—"

"Malcolm."

"Yes, well, he had heard about your relationship with Amelia Munroe—"

"The business one? That's the only one that concerns him," Geoff said.

"No. This one is with Auggie Munroe according to my sources. Anyway, Malcolm wants a sworn statement from you specifying that you will not be romantically involved with Amelia Munroe."

"I'm not signing that, so save yourself a trip." If he needed further proof that Malcolm Devonshire was an ass, he had it.

"You're backing yourself into a corner. If you don't sign it, you will lose all rights to your inheritance. That will nullify your half brothers' inheritance as well. Your father plans to ruin you if you ruin his plans, Geoff."

"Let him try. I'm my mother's son, Edmond, don't you ever forget that. My reputation is beyond reproach."

"Amelia's isn't," Edmond said.

He didn't like hearing Edmond threaten Amelia, and that was a threat, pure and simple. "Malcolm might be used to leaving women in his path like roadkill but I'm not. And I'm certainly not going to let you threaten her. I'm not signing any papers."

He hung up before Edmond could say anything else. He knew that his relationship with Amelia was going to have to either go to the next level or end, because the media and his biological father were doing their damnedest to tear them apart.

Amelia was surprised when she answered her door on Friday evening and found her brother standing there. He looked tired in his faded jeans and worn silk shirt. She stood there for a minute before stepping back to let him in.

"Do you have time for me?" Auggie asked.

That was the first time he'd ever asked her anything like that, and she wasn't sure what he wanted. She glanced at her watch. "I've got about forty minutes."

"Good. I talked to the board yesterday about your idea for making me the face of Munroe Hotels and they went for it. I am going to start by promoting the partnership agreement that you're working on with Everest Air."

"That's great, Auggie," she said. The board had of course already notified her but she didn't see any reason to tell him this.

"I'm here because I think that I should take over brokering the deal. I think that Devonshire will probably deal better with me man-to-man, and with you dating him, it doesn't seem appropriate for you to be doing business at the same time."

Amelia couldn't believe that this was coming from Auggie. "I'm not going to do anything to compromise the deal. And it's actually not official yet anyway."

"Fredrickson told me that unless you and I wanted to ruin the entire Munroe Hotels business, I need to step up and take control of this. Don't be upset," he said.

"I am. I've been running things behind the scenes for years and now because I'm dating Geoff, someone thinks I can't do it anymore? That's insulting."

"That's life," Auggie said.

"Men can be pigheaded."

Her brother laughed. "True, but until Fredrickson retires or gets booted off the board, there is little you or I can do about it."

Auggie sounded like he was ready to run the company for the first time in years. "You sound different."

"I am different now."

"Why? Does it have something to do with why you needed a week off?"

He shrugged. "I took time off because...well, let's just say I was dating someone but it didn't work out."

"A girl dumped you."

"Not a girl, Lia, *the* girl. And the only way I'm going to get her back is to straighten my life out."

"I'm glad to hear you say that. I hope you win her back," she said.

"I will. What about you and Geoff? Are you serious about him?"

"More serious than I've ever been before. But I have no idea if it's going to work out or not. I know that he doesn't like all the media attention and to be honest, I think I'm sick of it, too. But how do I make it go away?"

Auggie pulled her into a hug. "I have no idea. If you figure that one out, let me know."

"I will. Have you spoken to Father?" she asked. "About your new direction?"

"No. If I talk to him, he'll make me doubt myself. I think I need to do this on my own for once."

"I think so, too. If you need me, I'm here."

"I know you are. But I think I've leaned on you enough throughout our lives."

"I didn't mind it," she said. She liked knowing that she was the one who took care of Auggie. He was the one person in the world who'd always known what she really had to offer.

"My time's almost up. I think I'll go," he said. "Do you need anything from me?

"Two things, actually. Would you mind taking Lady Godiva for the weekend? I'm going out of town," she said. "I was going to have the dog-walking service take care of her, but I think she'd be happier with you."

"I don't mind at all. I could use the company," he said. "What else do you need?"

"One more week working on the deal with Everest Air. I'll finalize the terms we've been discussing, and then I'll turn it over to you."

"Okay," Auggie agreed. "But then you let me do my thing."

"Agreed."

A few minutes later he left with the dog in one arm. "Bye, sis."

"Bye, bro," she said as Auggie let himself out of her apartment.

She finished packing her bag for the weekend away with Geoff—she was meeting him in the parking garage in less than ten minutes. She was both looking forward to this weekend and dreading it.

She didn't know what his mother expected from her. This was the first time she'd met anyone's family. Normally the men she went out with were long gone from their families and lived in her world, the jet-set world where no one owed anyone any loyalty.

And that went double for her. But Geoff had a family and they wanted to meet her. She wondered if he was going to want to meet her family.

Doubt washed over her and she wondered what she was doing with Geoff. But she pushed it aside. When they were together, everything always felt right. She was with him because she liked the person she was in his eyes.

And he trusted her and believed in her. That's why they were doing business together. If he had any doubts, he never would have proposed the joint venture.

She liked the quiet moments that he found for them. And she loved the way he made her feel. He was in serious lust with her and she enjoyed every second of their lovemaking.

But that didn't mean that they belonged together or

that they'd last longer than it took for the passion to burn out between them, did it? What if she wasn't "the one" for him? She wanted to spend the rest of her days with Geoff and she was very afraid that no matter how things ended between them, she'd never be the same again.

She shook her head to clear out the thoughts—she was starting to drive herself crazy.

Amelia looked pensive when he picked her up. They didn't talk much as they drove out of the city. There were no cars following them, maybe because he was in a black Audi and not his flashy Veyron. Amelia was wearing a sexy outfit that was making it a little hard for him to focus. But he could tell something was wrong.

"What's on your mind?" he asked her once they were out of traffic and moving steadily along the highway.

"My brother stopped by tonight before you came to pick me up."

"And?"

"He talked to the board and he'll be taking over the partnership with Everest Air after we hammer out the details."

"Why?" Geoff asked carefully.

"The board didn't think it was appropriate for me to be dating you and doing business with you. I think they're afraid that if you dump me, the deal will fall through."

"That would never happen," he said.

"Dumping me or pulling out of the deal?" she asked.

He glanced over at her. She had large-framed black sunglasses on so he couldn't read her expression. But the tense way she held her body let him know that she was anxiously awaiting his answer.

"If our relationship ends, it's going to be because we both agreed that we'd taken it as far as we could."

She pushed her sunglasses up on her head and turned to face him. "Where do you see us heading?"

"I'm not sure. I just know that I don't like the thought of being without you."

"Me, too," she said. "When Auggie told me the board's concerns, I had to wonder if your own board wasn't saying the same thing to you."

Geoff shrugged, he knew if he told Amelia about Edmond's threats, she'd start to doubt herself and the business deal they'd carefully worked on. And Geoff knew he was more than capable of handling Edmond and Malcolm. Those two were mainly concerned about the bottom line, and as he'd told Edmond, he was his mother's son.

He'd ignore the media. With Amelia doing the same, they'd be okay. He didn't want to take a chance on doing something that would cause her to disappear. If Auggie took over the deal between their companies, it meant he wouldn't have a reason to see her all the time. And though the deal was being kept under wraps now, he wanted to let it out of the bag. He wanted to let the world see what kind of woman Amelia was and that she was his.

"I don't answer to anyone," he said.

"We all do."

"Everest Air is not the most important thing in the world to me."

"But it's your father's company."

"I never knew him. I still don't. He contacted me and the other heirs because he's dying."

"Oh, Geoff. I'm sorry. I didn't know he was sick. Does he want to make up for lost time?"

Geoff shook his head. "Hardly. He wants to make sure his company lives on long after he's gone."

She frowned at him. "God, that's cold. You deserve better than that from him."

"He's a stranger to me, so it doesn't bother me."

"Good. It's his loss. You're a fantastic man and I'm sure your brothers are as well. I can't believe he has never tried to get to know you all."

"His life was taking a different path," Geoff said. Hearing Amelia's perspective made him realize that he really had never needed Malcolm. He'd found his own way. The same way that Amelia had in her turbulent childhood.

"I'm glad our paths crossed," she said.

"You are? What made you say that?"

"I was thinking about how screwed up some parts of my life were before you. And I'm not saying this to add pressure to our relationship. But you have really given me some peace, and I enjoy it."

He reached over and took her hand in his, twining their fingers together as he continued to drive.

"You've brought excitement to mine," he said.

"Chaos you mean, right?"

Geoff brought her hand to his mouth and kissed the back of it before letting go. He didn't want to talk about how crazy her life was or how challenging he found it. He wanted to simply enjoy this weekend with her.

"I'm sorry," she said.

"Why?"

"You're trying to pretend that I haven't brought a headache into your life."

"I make my own decisions, Amelia," he said. "And I accept responsibility for them. Having you by my side is worth any of the problems that may have cropped up."

"Really? Sometimes I think it would be better for you if we just went back to our old lives. But I can't make myself do that."

"Good. I want you by my side," he said.

He knew that being with him and trying to avoid the paparazzi after a lifetime of engaging them must be taking a toll on her. He knew she was running around like a crazy woman to keep photographers from following her each time she met him. He appreciated the efforts she was making.

But at the same time he knew that they couldn't go on this way. He needed to find a way to permanently put an end to the media interference in their lives. He had no idea how to do it, but he could see the stress in Amelia and felt it himself each time they were confronted by a group of photographers.

He knew now how his cousins, the royal princes, felt. He'd often envied them, being the branch of the family to inherit the throne, but he couldn't live the way they did with their lives constantly under the scrutiny of everyone with nothing that was private.

As he entered the town of Bath, he had to slow down for traffic.

"I love Bath," Amelia said. "It's simply the prettiest place in England."

"I think some people would argue that, but I happen to agree."

He loved the lush green lawns, the flowing water of the Avon River that moved through the middle of town and the enchanting buildings. The influence of the Romans was still visible in the center of town near the legendary Roman baths. But the large medieval cathedral dominated the skyline of the city.

"How long have you had a house here?" she asked.

"Since my university days," he said. "I came here with one of my mates to visit his family and decided I wanted a home here as well. I wanted to come back often."

"And have you?"

"Yes, but this is the first time I've brought a woman here with me."

Amelia reached over to take his hand in hers and squeezed it tightly. "I'm flattered. And I'm sure I'm going to love it."

He was sure she would, too. And this weekend, he was determined to find a way to solidify his relationship with Amelia.

Eleven

Amelia had never expected to be so easily accepted into Geoff's family. His sisters were hilarious, treating him with love but also teasing the heck out of him. He was very much the patriarch of the family but he was indulgent as far as Gemma and Caroline were concerned.

Standing on the balcony overlooking the city of Bath on Sunday afternoon, she finally acknowledged that she had fallen in love with Geoff. It hadn't happened this weekend, she thought. No, it had started that very first night when he'd apologized for believing the worst of her. Then it had deepened when he'd kissed her in his car and made love to her on the rooftop, telling her that nothing mattered except what was between the two of them.

And everything that had happened since then had

just bound her more tightly to him, making her realize that he was everything she'd ever wanted in a man but had been afraid to reach out and take.

"So you like my brother?" Gemma said, appearing next to her.

"What makes you say that?" she asked.

"You are staring at him with stars in your eyes," Gemma said.

"That's embarrassing."

"Not really. I think he hung the moon, too. He's a bit arrogant but otherwise he's a great guy."

"He's bossy as hell," Amelia said.

Gemma sighed. "We've done our best but he simply won't listen to us. He still thinks he knows best."

"That's because I do," Geoff said, coming over to them and handing each of them a glass of Pimms.

"This is a girly conversation. Remember, you don't like those?" Gemma said.

"I'm interrupting it and changing it into a lovey-dovey conversation."

"See?" Gemma said looking at Amelia. "He's impossible."

"So are you, Gem."

His sister punched him playfully in the shoulder before walking away.

"I like your sisters," she said.

"They like you, too," he said. "My mum will be here in a short while. I should tell you something about her that I don't think I've mentioned. She's very afraid that I might treat you the way that Malcolm treated her. I think she'll want to speak to you."

"I'm not sure what to say. Why does she think that?" Amelia asked.

"I'm not entirely sure. But she said I should remember that even party girls have hearts that can be broken," Geoff said.

Amelia blinked. She knew she was going to like Geoff's mother. Any woman who would say that to her son had an inside knowledge of the world Amelia lived in.

"Everyone can be hurt," Amelia said, trying for a light tone. "Even business tycoons like yourself."

"Touché."

"Caro said that you warned her not to let her picture with Paul show up in *The Sun*."

"I did indeed. It's different with you and me," he said, clearly unashamed of the double standard he'd established for himself and his sisters.

"How?"

"We both know that I'm not just using you," he said.

"Maybe your sister knows the same thing about Paul."

He shrugged. "Until I'm certain of it, she's going to have to put up with my rules. I adore my sisters with their sassy attitudes. I don't want them to retreat from life because of men."

She understood exactly what he meant. "I'm glad they have you to look out for them. It'd be nice if everyone just dealt honestly with each other."

"Yes, it would," he said. "But that means trusting someone else not to hurt you, doesn't it?"

"Yes. That's the hard part," she admitted.

He hugged her with one arm. "I haven't betrayed your trust, have I?"

"No," she said.

"Amelia, there's something I need to discuss with you. It's about—"

"Geoff, darling, come and give your mother a hug."

Geoff pulled away without finishing, and Amelia could see he wanted to say more but now wasn't the time. He'd seemed concerned when he started to speak, but she had no clue what he'd wanted to say. Had she done something wrong? Was there some problem?

As she watched him with his mother, she realized that this was her secret dream. This family. A part of her felt that if she played her cards right, this could be her life. But another part felt insecure, like the other shoe was about to drop. Like she'd be lucky to make it through the weekend.

If he loved her, she thought, then everything would take care of itself. She just had to keep repeating that to herself.

Geoff wrapped his mum in a big bear hug and was surrounded by her slender arms and the scent of Chanel No. 5. It had long been her signature fragrance. Even though other designers had wanted to blend unique fragrances just for her, she preferred the one she'd worn as a young woman.

She wore a pair of wide-leg, camel-colored trousers and a fitted white blouse. Her auburn-colored hair was pulled back in a loose chignon and seeing her now, Geoff was struck by how pretty his mum was.

"Sorry to be late, darling," she said.

"Not a problem. I never mind waiting for you."

"That's good," she said with a smile.

"Mummy!" Caro said running over to them. "I can't wait for you to meet Paul. He's been eager for you to get here."

Paul joined them when Caro waved him over. He was an inch or two shorter than Geoff, and Geoff had used that to his advantage all afternoon, trying to intimidate the other man, but he'd stood his ground.

"Princess Louisa, it is a pleasure to meet you. Caro has told me so much about you," he said. He leaned in and gave her a kiss on the cheek.

"Please call me Louisa," his mother said.

"It would be my pleasure, Louisa."

Paul and his mum chatted as Geoff watched Amelia, waiting for the right moment to introduce her. She'd wandered over to Gemma and her date, Robert Tomlinson, the son of the current British prime minister.

As Geoff surveyed the balcony filled with his family, he realized that this was the life he wanted for all of them. He was tired of professional socializing and wanted to start having more time with his family and with Amelia.

He wanted the quiet domesticity that came with being a couple, and he wanted it soon. He was ready to be Amelia's. He just needed a signal from her that she wanted it, too.

For all he knew she would miss her wild lifestyle. He knew he kept her more than satisfied in bed, but there was more to life than that.

Realizing that her happiness was his chief concern sobered him up.

"She's a stunningly beautiful girl," his mum said as she came up to him.

"Yes, she is. You can't help but notice her when she's in a room."

"I can see that. What does she mean to you?" she asked.

"Mum, I've told you, I don't want to talk about my intentions with you. Not yet."

Louisa nodded. "I know you said that but I want to make sure you have more of me in you than Malcolm."

"There is no way to prove that to you," he said.

"I know, darling," she said, patting his arm. "I didn't mean that the way it sounded."

This had always been an issue between them. At times he wondered if Malcolm even knew what kind of wreckage he'd left behind when he'd abandoned Geoff's mother.

"Speaking of him, have you had a call from Ainsley Patterson or her assistant?"

Louisa took a deep breath. "I have. She wants to interview me and the other women."

"Are you going to do it?"

"Do you want me to?" she asked. "I really don't want to, but I also don't want to be the only one who doesn't participate."

"From what I understand, Steven's mother is reluctant to do it as well."

"The physicist, right?"

"Yes, Mum. I spoke to Ainsley and she assured me

that the piece is going to focus on all three of you from a fashion perspective."

She shook her head. "I'm still considering it. I know that it will mean publicity for the company but I really don't think we need any more money."

He smiled. Whoever had tried to use money as a reason for her to do the interview had made a huge mistake. His mother had more money than Midas and didn't think that was a justification for anything.

"If you don't want to do it, we can both walk away."

"You'd do that for me?"

"Of course I would, Mum."

"Thank you, Geoff," she said.

"Now where is Amelia?"

"I'm here," Amelia said, walking over to them.

He'd already started to figure out how much he loved Amelia, but seeing that shy smile on her face as she approached his mother simply confirmed it. He wanted to go to her and kiss her because he wasn't sure he could tell her how he felt, but he sure as hell could show her.

"Hello, Amelia," his mum said.

"Princess Louisa."

"Please call me Louisa."

"I have to tell you that you have raised three wonderful kids. The girls are very sweet and funny, and Geoff is simply the best date a girl could have."

He arched one eyebrow at Amelia's comment and she winked at him.

"Thank you, darling," Louisa said. "My kids *are* spectacular."

"They share your modesty," Amelia said with a laugh.

Louisa laughed along with her. "I like this girl, Geoff."

"Me, too, Mum."

"Now leave us alone for some girl talk," Louisa said.

"Very well," Geoff said. He reached around his mother and pulled Amelia into his arms and kissed her.

"You mean the world to me," he whispered before he left them to chat.

Louisa put her arm through Amelia's and led her off the balcony and out into the backyard where they could be alone.

"I hope you don't mind me pulling you away from the party," she said.

"Not at all. I wanted to talk to you as well. I'm so sorry about the photos that keep showing up of Geoff and me."

Louisa shook her head. "That's not your fault. Geoff's a big boy. He knows how to deal with the media."

"Ignore them?"

"Well, that has worked for us, but I think you have a different policy, don't you?"

"I do. I use them to keep my name in the public spotlight. It helps when I'm trying to promote the hotel chain or one of the charities I work with. But now...well, now that I'm involved with Geoff, they do seem to be in the way."

"I was like you once. Just living my life and enjoying every second of it. But everything has consequences."

"Of course. You should know that Geoff is a great guy. He's always treated me well."

Amelia knew that Louisa was trying to look out for her and it was important to Amelia that Geoff's mother realize what a wonderful man he was. He'd never tried to use her or treat her with anything other than respect.

"I know, he's a good boy. He always was. But the world we live in can change a man. Do you know that I was engaged to Malcolm?"

"No. I didn't know that. In fact, I know very little about your relationship."

"Well, when the news of it started circulating, that was when he started panicking. I think he was afraid I'd try to change him. To be fair, I probably would have, but who can really say."

Amelia understood. "My parents had a very tumultuous marriage."

"Are they divorced?"

Amelia laughed. "No. But they don't live together. Their passion is somewhat…all-consuming."

"Ah. So they can't give each other up but they can't live together either?"

"Exactly."

"Is that what you have with my son?"

Amelia tried to find the right words while they strolled through the beautifully landscaped backyard. "No. We have passion, but there is also peace. I don't know if this will make sense, Louisa, but my entire life has been very chaotic and being with Geoff just makes me happy."

Louisa squeezed her hand. "That makes perfect sense, darling. I think that is exactly as it should be."

"I'm so glad you think so," Amelia said, relieved.

Louisa stopped walking. "I need some advice and you might be the only woman I know who can understand this situation. I've been asked to do an interview with a fashion magazine, along with the two other mistresses of Malcolm's. They want to do a fashion retrospective and talk about how we are all uniquely different. I've always avoided things like that, but I think using the media now to show that I'm not a victim might be a good idea."

Amelia wasn't sure what to say. "I've always thought of the media as working for me. I try to get them to picture me the way I want them to. If I were you, I'd do it, but I'd do it on my own terms."

Louisa nodded. "I have been thinking I should do it because I believe I'm the only holdout. They'd probably paint me in a very unflattering light."

Amelia shook her head. "How could anyone do that to you? Everyone knows how much work you do with charities, and how you took your deceased husband's fortune and used it to fund an organization that helps unwed mothers."

She flushed. "That's only money. I have a lot of that, and a lot of time to give."

Before she could say anything else, Paul, Caro and Gemma walked into the backyard. Paul had a football in his hands and the girls were both laughing at something he'd said. Robert and Geoff were right behind them, carrying trays of food and drinks.

"Want to play a game of kick around?" Paul asked.

"Louisa, Caro told me you taught her to play when she was little."

"I did indeed. I taught Geoff and Gemma as well. I was an accomplished player when I was younger."

"After we eat, you can show us if you still have it, Mum," Gemma said.

Everyone worked together to get the meal ready and they had nice luncheon. Then it was time for "kick around," as Paul called it. Amelia wasn't very athletic, something that everyone noticed the first time she tried to kick the ball and missed.

Geoff came over to her and wrapped his arms around her from behind. "Do you need some lessons?"

"Yes," she said. "I'm afraid soccer isn't my sport."

"Maybe that's the problem, you Yank. We call it football over here."

He put his hands on her waist and bent his legs behind hers, pulling her fully against him. She forgot all about the ball. Geoff was saying something to her, but all she could think about was how good he felt.

"Ready?" he asked.

She shook her head.

He tipped her head back and kissed her quick. "Just try to keep your body limber."

She nodded and the ball came careening toward her again across the very green lawn. She caught it, dropped it and kicked it to Caro.

"I got it."

"You cheated," Gemma said. "You can't use your hands! I've seen five-year-olds with better skills than you."

Amelia smiled at her. "I'm not very athletic."

"No, you're not," Geoff said. "But I wouldn't change a thing about you."

His words warmed her. For a few minutes, she had that floating feeling that came when everything was right in her world. Though she felt accepted by Geoff's mother and sisters and finally admitted to herself that she loved him, she knew that things weren't resolved between them. Geoff was keeping something from her. And she knew that it had to be something big, because he'd tried to talk to her twice and each time he'd been pulled away she saw a look in his eyes that told her time was running out.

Twelve

Amelia sat on the balcony watching the sun set over the city of Bath while Geoff was downstairs dealing with business. Malcolm's attorney had mysteriously arrived ten minutes after his family had left. She knew Edmond through Cecelia, but the man barely even glanced at her when he arrived. Geoff looked angry, so she'd excused herself before he could ask her to.

She was tired, but it wasn't a bad feeling. She really felt like the weekend had changed her perspective on life. Louisa had been a breath of fresh air and a solid example that loving and losing didn't mean giving up on life. The woman might avoid the spotlight, but she vibrated with a joie de vivre that Amelia hoped she still had when she was in her fifties.

She'd brought the pitcher of Pimms mixed with fizzy lemonade and cut-up fruit out on the balcony with her.

She was reclining on one of the solid wood loungers with a thick, red-striped cushion and a soft down pillow at the top.

She was a little chilly as the sun set but wrapped a cashmere scarf around her shoulders. The lights of the city started to come on and she thought that she could be happy in this quiet, small town.

Though Bath wasn't a tiny little burg, it was removed from the hustle and bustle of London and though she knew there were paparazzi in the area since many Hollywood celebrities had houses here, they seemed to steer clear of Geoff's estate.

"Sorry about that," Geoff said, stepping out onto the balcony. "I wasn't expecting that to take as long as it did." He looked strange, as though his mind were still on whatever business he'd been discussing.

"I didn't mind sitting here. I was enjoying the quiet tonight."

"Was it too loud today with everyone?"

"Not at all. I really like your family. They are exactly what I always dreamed I'd have when I was visiting someone else's house. For a few moments today, it felt like your family was mine, too."

"I loved sharing my family with you."

"Thank you, Geoff." She waited for him to continue, but he was quiet. She was tempted to ask him what he'd been about to tell her earlier, but she couldn't bring herself to do it.

Geoff sat down on her lounger by her legs, facing her. He lifted her legs over his lap.

"Amelia, we have a good thing. I only know that right now this is working and I don't want it to end."

"Neither do I. You have become important to me. I'm not sure how that happened because I vowed to myself that you weren't going to get the better of me."

Geoff smiled down at her and it was easy for her to see the caring in his eyes. She felt lit from within when he looked at her like that.

"I think I've had the very best of you," he said.

"You have," she said as he leaned in to kiss her.

"We'd better pack up and get going. I have a pretty busy week," Geoff said.

Her mellow feeling started to wane. She knew this was just the reality of two very busy people getting together. She had her life and he had his.

"I guess I should get my things together," she said, starting to rise. He stopped her, and her breath caught.

"Amelia?"

"Yes?" she said.

"Will you live with me?" he asked.

Live with him? She wasn't sure she was ready for that. But at the same time she was entranced with the idea. She wanted to spend more time with him and this might be the right move. Except that she wasn't sure.

"Can I think about it for a few days?"

"What's to think about, Amelia?"

"I'm just not sure. I'm not trying to be difficult," she said.

He leaned in closer to her. "What are you afraid of?"

"Needing you," she said.

"You'll have me. I'm not going anywhere."

"For now," she said, studying his expression.

"If I made you a promise, would you believe me?" he asked.

"I don't know," she admitted quietly.

"Let's give it a try. We'll spend a few nights at each other's places first and see what happens."

She wanted to say yes, realizing that if she were going to let fear motivate her, then she wasn't going to have a very good life.

"Okay. But you'll have to stay with me. I have my dog."

He let out a laugh, and for a moment the concern behind his eyes vanished. "No problem. Do you want to set up specific days?"

"Not if you're going to laugh at me."

"I'm not, I swear. Monday, Wednesday and Friday?"

"Next weekend I'm scheduled to fly to Paris to speak at a conference."

"I'll check my schedule. If I'm free I'll come to Paris with you. Unless you'd rather be alone."

"No, I'd love to have you with me," she said.

Planning for the future made her feel like they were a real couple. She was scared to trust in that but she decided that for right now, she was going to. There was no other solution that was going to work.

She was already in love with Geoff. Now she'd be able to figure out if she could live with him. She'd just have to trust that whatever was bothering him would come out sooner or later. If he was asking to live with her, then it probably had nothing to do with her, she told herself.

* * *

Geoff wasn't the kind of man who liked to leave loose ends and "living" with Amelia felt like a loose end. He had met with both her and Auggie earlier in the day and he'd wanted to make their arrangement official, but she'd been cool and businesslike, probably because her board didn't want to see any untoward behavior from her.

Edmond had left another warning message on his voice mail and frankly, Geoff was sick of the older gentleman. There was no contest in his mind between Amelia and Everest Air. He'd always pick Amelia.

Edmond had not been too pleased with that but Geoff didn't back down and he knew the profit he was increasing at the airline had helped to sway the older gentleman. Geoff wasn't Malcolm and Amelia hadn't made him lose interest in his business. It had in fact made him even more determined to succeed so that their joint venture would be profitable and help her out as well.

His secretary reminded him that he had the fund-raising dinner that night with Mary Werner. He called Mary to confirm that they were still on and then called Amelia to let her know he'd be home late.

"This is Amelia," she said by way of greeting.

"It's Geoff."

"Hey there, sexy."

"Hello back," he said. "I have to attend the breast cancer function tonight, so I'm going to get to your place late."

He heard the sound of rustling papers on her end. "I think I have something...yes, a dinner party. Do you want me to stop by the event on my way home? We are one of the corporate sponsors of the event—Munroe Foundation, I mean."

"No, that's fine. I'll just look forward to seeing you when I'm home."

"That will be better. Then I can have you all to myself," she said.

"I like the sound of that," Geoff replied.

"Do you?" she asked.

"Yes, I do. I am going to like seeing you almost every day," he admitted.

"I'll be home by ten."

"I'll try to get there then as well."

"That's my other line. I have to go." She hung up before he could say another word.

When he picked Mary up at her place for their evening, he wished he were picking up Amelia instead. As he rang her bell, he thought he saw someone behind him, but when he glanced up and down the street, he saw nothing.

"Hello, Geoff," Mary said when she opened the door to her Notting Hill town house. She looked nice in her pink dress. He leaned in to give her a kiss and thought he heard a click behind him. When he turned around, all he saw was a man walking his dog at the end of the street.

He shook his head. He was getting paranoid because of the photographers who always followed Amelia around. "Are you ready to go?"

"Let me grab my purse," she said.

A few minutes later they were seated in his Audi, driving toward the event, which was being held at the Munroe Hotel. He pulled up and tossed his keys to the valet. Then he gave Mary his arm as they walked into the hotel. There was a red carpet leading to the ballroom and lots of people taking pictures as they entered.

"Thank you for escorting me tonight, Geoff."

"No problem. This event is important."

Mary nodded. "This is one of your mother's causes, isn't it?"

"I think it is every woman's cause. Since I have a mother and two sisters, it is important to me."

Mary smiled over at him. "Shall we get a drink and hit the dance floor?"

Geoff didn't want to hold any woman other than Amelia, but one dance with Mary didn't seem like it was too much to ask.

"Okay, let's go."

"To this song?" she said with a bit of surprise in her voice. The song was Pink's "Who Knew."

"I'm not much of a fast dancer," Mary said.

"Let's give it a try. I bet you'll be pretty good at it," he said, realizing that with Mary she just needed some gentle encouragement.

She gave him an excited grin and stood up. "Okay. Let's do it."

They hit the dance floor as the music changed to another upbeat number, this one by Steph Cordo, an act his half brother Henry was producing for Everest Records. They danced to her song, and at the end they transitioned into the new John Mayer song.

"Yes, a slow dance," Mary said giving him a very hopeful look.

"Okay, one dance," he said.

She stepped closer to him and he put one hand on her

waist and held her hand in his other one. They danced well together, which surprised him. On the dance floor, he saw another side to Mary. After several songs, he paid her compliment.

"You should dance more often, Mary. It brings out another side to your personality."

"You think so?"

"Definitely," he said.

"Devonshire," someone called. He glanced over to see a rather shabby-looking photographer with an expensive, professional camera around his neck.

The man snapped a picture of Geoff and Mary, and then disappeared into the crowd. Geoff went after him, but by the time he got through the crowd, the man was gone. This would be fodder for Edmond and Malcolm and the papers, but he'd handle it.

He tried to tell himself the photo was nothing and he wasn't going to worry about it, but he feared that Amelia might see things differently. When he got back to the table, Mary was acting like a gracious hostess to the others there.

"I have to go," he said.

"I understand. I'm going to stay a bit longer and I'll catch a cab home," Mary said.

He nodded and left the hotel, intent on getting to Amelia before any more damage was done.

Amelia was having a good night out. Bebe was a guest at Dominic Regenti's dinner party as well, so she'd been hanging out with her friend, drinking lovely fruity cocktails and talking about Geoff all evening.

"He sent me flowers today at my office. Did I tell you that?"

"About a dozen times," Bebe said.

"That was really sweet. They are the same flowers that are hanging from baskets on the streets of Bath. We walked all over the city and no one paid any attention to us. It was so nice," Amelia said.

Bebe put her arm though Amelia's and said, "I know, I know. It was an enchanted weekend, something that didn't even feel real."

"Am I babbling?" Amelia asked her friend.

"Only the slightest bit and I don't mind at all. I think you are in love."

"I think I am, too," Amelia said.

Dominic sat down next to her. "You are what?"

Dominic was one of her dearest friends. His party was small and intimate—just her and Bebe, and Dominic and Lucinda, his wife. Dominic and Amelia had met years earlier at one of Amelia's mother's fashion shows. He was fifteen years older than Amelia, and he'd been there with one of his mistresses. That was aeons before he'd met Lucinda and settled down.

"Don't say anything until I'm back in the room," Lucinda called from the kitchen. She was bringing dessert into the sitting room.

Lucinda was a celebrity chef who had gotten her start working in Gordon Ramsay's kitchen. On one of his early shows her charisma and beauty had been spotted by one of the producers and she'd been offered her own show. That was when Dominic had started courting her.

"Okay, here I am," she said, carrying a tray with champagne Jell-O and whipped cream.

Dominic stood up, took the tray from his wife and gave her a kiss on the cheek. "Let me take that."

"You guys are so sweet," Amelia said.

"We are," Lucinda agreed. "So what about your man? We want to hear about Geoff."

"I'm not sure what to say. He's…" She trailed off, realizing she didn't know how to talk about him without revealing how she felt. Or sounding foolish. She was still afraid of being hurt.

"He sent her flowers at her office today. The same ones that were hanging in baskets in Bath," Bebe said, "which is where they were this weekend."

"He wanted to remind you of the time you spent together," Lucinda said. "Why don't you do that, Dominic?"

He tugged Lucinda down on his lap as she handed the last dessert out. "Because you are allergic to flowers, my love."

She kissed him on the cheek. "That is right."

"He also sent me a mask from Botswana, which is where we first met. He'd noticed that I'd admired it, I think," Amelia said.

"That is good. What else does he notice?" Lucinda asked.

"Everything. When I'm with him, I feel like I'm the only woman on the planet."

Dominic smiled at her and she saw that he was happy for her. "It's about time you found a man like that. Why didn't you bring him with you tonight?"

"He had a function to attend. He's as busy as I am

but I think we are starting to merge our calendars and spend more time together."

"That is the hard part," Lucinda said. "Dominic travels a lot and that was a big struggle in the beginning of our relationship."

"Yes, it was, because she was stubborn and wouldn't quit her job to go with me."

"I'm glad she didn't. That was not nice of you to ask her to give up her career for you," Bebe said.

"Hey, I offered her a lot of money to be my personal chef."

"I hope you said no, Lucinda," Bebe said.

"She did, of course. But eventually I brought her around to my way of thinking."

Amelia laughed at her friends. As they bantered and had their dessert, she realized that she missed Geoff. She missed having him at her side, enjoying the evening with her.

Being in love was more than just a feeling, she thought. It was also the fact that she wanted to spend every moment of the day with him. And of course the nights. If he'd been here, he would have fit in well with Dominic and Lucinda. She wanted him to become integrated completely into her life and she wasn't going to be happy until he was.

Happy, she thought. She'd never gotten to the point where she felt safe being happy. She was afraid to trust that what she had with Geoff was going to last, and that wasn't fair, she thought. Not to herself, and not to Geoff. She couldn't wait to get home and tell him.

She wasn't going to hide the fact that she loved him anymore. She wanted the life that Dominic and Lucinda had together and running away from love wasn't the key to that kind of deep-seated happiness.

She left Dominic's a little after ten, which was later than she'd thought she'd be. She and Bebe shared a cab. When Bebe got out of the car, she gave Amelia a hug and Amelia sat back in the seat as the cabbie took her home. She had a bubble of excitement in the pit of her stomach as she got closer to her house where she hoped Geoff was waiting for her.

Thirteen

Amelia got out of the cab and walked toward the entrance of her apartment building. She noticed that Tommy had company this evening and she smiled at the men as she walked past them. She heard them calling her name and asking about Geoff, but she didn't pay the least bit of attention to them.

Taking a page from Geoff's family's book, she'd decided to start ignoring them and it felt good. The bellman held the door for her and she thanked him as she walked by.

The elevator was empty when she swiped her key card and took it up to her penthouse. And as she walked into her apartment, she felt a thrill to see Geoff standing in the living area on his cell phone.

He hung up when he saw her and turned to face her. She saw that look again—something was wrong.

"How was your evening?" he asked.

"Fun, but I missed you, Geoff," she said. "I didn't realize until tonight just how much a part of my life you've become." She wanted to know what he had to say, but not before he knew exactly how she felt.

"You've become very important to me as well," he said.

She dropped her purse on the floor and Godiva trotted out to sniff it. Amelia bent down and petted her adorable little dog before sending her back to her padded bed.

Then she walked over to Geoff. She wrapped her arms around him, resting her head on his chest. Geoff's arms came around her and he held her very tightly to him.

"We need to talk."

She tipped her head back, panic settling in her throat. "Right now? I was hoping that you'd scoop me up and take me to bed. I want you to make love to me."

His pupils dilated and she felt his erection stir against her belly. "I'd like nothing more, but—"

She silenced him with the most passionate kiss she could muster. Finally, he lifted her into his arms and carried her down the hall to her bedroom. He set her on her feet next to the bed. With Geoff she felt exotic in a good way.

She wrapped her arms around his neck and pulled his mouth down to hers, kissing him with all the love she'd kept bottled inside. His mouth opened over hers and she couldn't get enough of him.

She pulled him closer to her and reached for the tie around his neck. For a moment, it seemed like he would try to stop her, but she loosened the knot and pulled it free. She felt his hands on her back and soon he was whispering in her ear, which inflamed her even more.

He found the zipper in the side of her blouse and undid it. She whipped the silk fabric over her head and tossed it on the floor. Reaching for his buttons and undoing them as quickly as her fingers would allow, she fumbled over the middle button.

"Get naked," he said, his voice ragged and almost harsh.

She took off her bra and then unzipped her skirt and pushed it down her legs, along with her panties. She stepped out of her heels and turned to drop her clothing on the floor. Geoff came up behind her.

His naked body pressed all along her back. His hands came up to cup her breasts and tweak her nipples. His hard manhood pressed into her butt and she moved her hips, stroking him with her backside.

He dropped kisses along the length of her neck and she felt his teeth against her skin. She wanted more.

"I need you."

"Amelia," he said. "I need you, too."

He bent her forward and she braced her arms against the bed as he widened his stance behind her. She felt him at the entrance to her body and she tightened and pulsed in anticipation. He cupped her breasts in both his hands and then entered her slowly from behind.

When he was fully seated she almost came. He was so deep and as he thrust in and out of her, she felt everything so much more intensely than she ever had before.

He slid one hand down her body though the thin curls between her legs and stroked the center of her pleasure as he continued to thrust in and out of her.

He leaned in low over her and she felt him pressed all along her back, his hands between her legs and on her breasts. She was completely surrounded by him. Her world narrowed and focused until it was only Geoff.

She felt everything in her body tightening and she called his name as her orgasm rolled through her. A minute later Geoff cried out as he came, filling her with his essence. He fell down on the bed, keeping them connected and holding her close to him. Sweat dried on their bodies as their breathing slowed.

"I love you," she said before she could stop herself.

Geoff's eyes widened. He pulled her back into his arms and made love to her again until they were both exhausted. As they fell asleep, she couldn't shake the thought that Geoff hadn't said he loved her back.

Geoff woke to the sun shining and the smell of coffee from the kitchen. He was in the bed of a woman who'd confessed to loving him last night. He took a moment to savor this before a sick feeling settled in the pit of his stomach as he realized he'd left loose ends last night. Someone had taken a photo of him with Mary and he needed to tell Amelia before she saw it. And that wasn't all he needed to tell her.

He heard her phone ring. A minute later, his mobile phone started ringing. He glanced at the caller ID and saw that it was Edmond. He jumped out of bed, grabbed his pants and yanked them on as he tried to run into the kitchen.

Amelia was standing in the doorway with her little dog dancing at her feet. She was pale and she stared hard at him. She held a copy of *The Sun* in one hand and as he walked toward her she shook her head.

"How could you do this?"

"I can explain," he started to say as his eyes fell on the front page.

There was a photo of him kissing Amelia on the streets of Bath with a caption that read "Sunday?" Next to that was a photo of him kissing Mary hello at her door, and one of them dancing. The caption read "Monday?" The headline read, "Devonshire Playboy Bests Trashy Heiress at Her Own Game."

"What is this, Geoff?"

He took the paper from her and sat down, running his hand through his hair. "I should have told you right away."

"Told me what?"

"That Mary was my date last night."

Amelia had tears in her eyes. He wanted to take back what he had just said. He hurt her, and that wasn't his intent.

"It's was nothing with Mary. She and I had plans to attend the function before I even knew you, but of course the media is trying to make it into something it's not."

"I'm not jealous of Mary Werner," Amelia said. "If you want to spend your time with her, that's fine with me. But do me the courtesy of at least letting me know that you have a date with another woman."

"I—"

"Don't! Please don't try to justify this or explain it to me. I'm not…"

"Not what?"

"Not some party girl you can have an exotic thrill with and then cast aside. I asked you about Mary, remember?"

Geoff shook his head. "I'm not casting you aside. I asked you to move in with me."

"It's not enough. Now I know why you couldn't tell me you loved me last night… I thought the words might be hard for you to say, but now I know this is just a game to you."

"That is not true. Don't let your temper get the better of you."

"Stop trying to calm me down," she said, sparks in her eyes. "I'm so mad at you right now."

"I'm sorry."

She shook her head. "That's not enough. I need you to leave. I don't want to lay eyes on you ever again."

"Too bad…I'm not walking away that easily," he said.

"Your life—our life is not a crazy circus. This is a sensationalized story to try to sell papers. You know that I wouldn't go from one woman's bed to yours."

She started to argue, but then stopped. "You're right. I do know that. But I'm not sure I can hold my head up while the rest of the city believes I'm part of the Devonshire legacy."

"No one believes this crap."

"Yes, they do," she said. Her phone rang again. "We can't keep seeing each other."

"Why not?"

"Because I love you, you idiot, and I can't stand to see a photo of you with another woman. And this won't be the last one. No matter what you do or where you go someone will always be following you trying to find the evidence that you are just like Malcolm."

He was starting to get angry with her. "I'm not Malcolm. And I've never treated you with anything but respect."

"You look like Malcolm," she said. "And you're the

star of the gossip rags this morning with two different women. Are the comparisons starting to add up in your mind?"

"You aren't being rational," he said.

"I am. I'm just not saying anything that you want to hear. But it makes sense. You know as well as I do that ignoring this isn't going to make it go away."

"I don't know that and neither do you. What I know, Amelia, is that you don't even want to try. That you are letting fear guide this decision."

"Fear? Of what?"

"Of finally being with a man who isn't going to let you scare him off with your 'outrageous' behavior. I think you're afraid to live a normal, quiet life. You were probably waiting for this to happen so you could use it as an excuse to cut me out of your life."

His mobile was ringing nonstop; he ignored the calls from his sisters, but his mother wasn't someone he could send to voice mail. When Amelia picked up her dog and walked out of the room, he answered the call from his mother.

"Mum, this is Geoff."

"I'm…I don't know what to say to you. How could you do that to Amelia?"

"It's not what it looks like," he said, trying to defend himself.

"I'm sure in your eyes it isn't. But this behavior is unacceptable and I have no choice but to disown you."

"Mother, don't be dramatic."

"I'm not. You have sisters, Geoff. I raised you to be a gentleman—"

"I *am* a gentleman, Mum. I will fix this."

"You had better. I'm going to call Amelia later. This is…I'm so upset with you, Geoff."

"I know."

He hung up the phone and it rang again, this time it was Edmond.

"Devonshire."

"I guess you've seen the papers this morning."

"Indeed. Did you do this?"

"No. You were managing the heiress and your line of business very well. Why did you add another woman to the mix?"

Geoff realized that what Amelia had said was true. Everyone was going to believe he was simply another Devonshire male who couldn't be satisfied with one woman.

"I didn't. Listen, I need to sort this out with Amelia. She is more important to me than you or Malcolm."

"Is she?" Edmond asked.

"She is. And I have to figure out how to handle this."

"Good luck, sir. I think you will need it."

Geoff knew he wasn't going to be able to fix things right away, and he frankly had no idea what to do. He left her apartment and walked through a flurry of paparazzi—and the idea came to him.

He drew Tommy aside and asked the man to take a picture of him later that day. Then he went home and called his half brothers so they would know what he planned to do.

"I think you're a nutter," Henry said. "But love does that to the best of us."

Love. He'd never thought he'd admit to it, but losing

Amelia made him desperate and he knew that he'd loved her since he'd first clapped eyes on her. "Love will."

"I hate to say it but I agree," Steven said. "I flew to New York when I could have sent my VP and suffered through jet lag just to have a drink with Ainsley."

Geoff laughed and was glad he'd found these brothers. "Are you sure the publicity will be okay?"

"Definitely," Henry said.

"Of course," Steven chimed in. "We need to right the wrongs that Malcolm perpetrated when he abandoned our mothers. Show the world that Devonshire men know how to treat ladies."

"I agree."

He ended the call with his brothers. Now it felt good to call them that. He looked at the sign he'd made and went downstairs and drove his Veyron across town to her apartment building.

Good to his word, Tommy waited out front. Geoff knew this could all backfire, but he also knew that if he didn't take a chance on love with Amelia he'd miss out on the greatest adventure of his life.

He got out of the car and left his suit jacket behind. He held the poster board with the message he'd written on it. Tommy snapped pictures as he walked to the building. And Geoff held up his sign.

"Make sure this gets in *The Sun* tomorrow," Geoff said, handing the man some folded bills.

"I will."

Geoff didn't like the thought of leaving, but he knew that now was the time to wait. So he got in his Veyron and left, hoping tomorrow Amelia would see the papers and put him out of his misery.

* * *

Bebe had arrived shortly after Geoff had left and she stayed the night. They'd drank martinis and talked and cried. Amelia took comfort from her but Bebe couldn't stop the hurt.

Amelia's mobile rang and she glanced at the caller ID. "Hey, Auggie."

"Lia, are you okay? I saw this morning's paper and I'm not sure what to say. I'm ready to end the deal with Everest Air. I mean, no one treats you like he did."

"Thank you, Auggie, but business comes first. This could be your last chance with the board."

"No, sis, you come first. I know I haven't been a great big brother but I'm ready to make up for lost time."

"Auggie, that's so sweet."

"I mean it," he said. "But seeing *The Sun* this morning made me hesitate to call and cancel the deal. Have you seen it?"

"No," she said. She turned to Bebe. "Will you run to the corner kiosk and get *The Sun?*"

"I will."

Bebe left and Auggie hung up. Amelia sat on her couch with her little dog, holding her close and wondering why it was that she kept going after the one thing that she knew she couldn't have. She should have kept her feelings to herself.

But not saying she loved Geoff out loud wouldn't have made the emotions not exist. She did love him and she missed him.

"Oh, my God," Bebe said as she came back into the apartment fifteen minutes later. "Look at this."

Bebe brought the paper to Amelia and she glanced at the photo there. It was Geoff and he held a sign in his hand...*Sunday, Monday and every other day of the week, I love Amelia Munroe.*

She put her hand to her mouth, afraid to believe what she was seeing.

"He's downstairs," Bebe said.

"Who is?"

"Geoff. He told me he wants to see you. Will you let him up?"

"I don't know. What should I do?"

Bebe hugged her close and then stood up. "Listen to the man. You fell in love with him, so he must be something special."

Bebe left and a few minutes later the doorbell rang. She put Godiva down and walked over to answer it. Geoff stood in the doorway, looking as if he hadn't slept a wink all night.

"Can I come in?"

She nodded and stepped back.

"Did you see the paper?" he asked.

"Yes. But that doesn't change anything."

"I love you, Amelia. That changes everything."

She wanted to believe him but her heart was still vulnerable after yesterday, and she was afraid to trust him. "As long as we are together the paps are going to be parked downstairs. They are going to keep on waiting to see what we do next. To try to find some story—because to the world, we don't make sense."

"You make sense to me," he said.

"It's not enough."

Geoff started to sweat. He knew that writing his feelings on a sign for the world to see was one thing, telling Amelia how he felt was another thing entirely. He wasn't sure he wanted her to know that he was vulnerable where she was concerned. That she was the weakness he'd hoped to keep the world from seeing.

He hadn't realized he could love someone the way he loved Amelia. And that scared him.

"I care about you."

The words came out in a rush and weren't at all rehearsed. He was a man who always knew what to say and when to say it, but now, faced with losing the one woman he didn't want to let go of, he couldn't string together a decent sentence.

"I know you do, but that's not enough."

Geoff shook his head. "You are bold and brash and you live your life by your own standards. And…I love you."

"What?"

"You heard me. And I'm not walking out of your door this morning to leave you alone. We are going to spend the rest of our lives together."

"Do you mean that, Geoff?"

"Yes," he said. He walked across the room and pulled her into his arms. "I'm not about to let you go, Amelia Munroe. You are the best thing that has ever happened to me."

She hugged him close. Not saying a word as he held her, he rocked them back and forth. He knew he had a lot of things to get sorted but he was determined to keep Amelia Munroe and make her his wife.

They spent the next month planning their wedding. Geoff attended every public event that she did and was always at her side, touching her and kissing her. And without their releasing a statement or saying a word to the media, the stories started to change. Soon they were called the most romantic couple of the year.

Amelia's mother designed her wedding dress and the invitations were sent out. Bebe was to be the maid of honor and Geoff decided to ask Paul to be his best man. He knew that Caro and Paul were a serious item.

Geoff, Steven and Henry all received a telegram two days before Geoff's wedding that Malcolm had died.

Geoff didn't know how the other men felt, but he had a moment of sadness that he'd never had the chance to really get to know Malcolm.

Steven was declared the winner of the competition that Malcolm had laid for his three heirs. And Geoff and Henry were both given the option of staying on as the CEOs of their business units, something they both accepted.

The morning of the wedding dawned clear and sunny, and Geoff woke his bride by making love to her. Eight hours later she was still glowing as she walked down the aisle toward him.

Choppers flew over the country estate where they were being married and a famous photographer took pictures of them, but Geoff and Amelia both knew that they wouldn't need pictures to remember this moment or this day.

As they shared their first dance together, Amelia looked up at Geoff and reminded him of the promises he'd made to her.

"I would never break a promise to you, Amelia," he said. "I love you too much."

* * * * *

Harlequin offers a romance for every mood!
See below for a sneak peek from
our suspense romance line
Silhouette® Romantic Suspense.
Introducing HER HERO IN HIDING
by New York Times *bestselling author Rachel Lee.*

Kay Young returned to woozy consciousness to find that she was lying on a soft sofa beneath a heap of quilts near a cheerfully burning fire. When she tried to move, however, everything hurt, and she groaned.

At once she heard a sound, then a stranger with a hard, harsh face was squatting beside her. "Shh," he said softly. "You're safe here. I promise."

"I have to go," she said weakly, struggling against pain. "He'll find me. He can't find me."

"Easy, lady," he said quietly. "You're hurt. No one's going to find you here."

"He will," she said desperately, terror clutching at her insides. "He always finds me!"

"Easy," he said again. "There's a blizzard outside. No one's getting here tonight, not even the doctor. I know, because I tried."

"Doctor? I don't need a doctor! I've got to get away."

"There's nowhere to go tonight," he said levelly. "And if I thought you could stand, I'd take you to a window and show you."

But even as she tried once more to pull away the quilts, she remembered something else: this man had been gentle when he'd found her beside the road, even when she had kicked and clawed. He hadn't hurt her.

Terror receded just a bit. She looked at him and detected signs of true concern there.

The terror eased another notch and she let her head sag on the pillow. "He always finds me," she whispered.

"Not here. Not tonight. That much I can guarantee."

Will Kay's mysterious rescuer protect her from her worst fears?
Find out in HER HERO IN HIDING by
New York Times *bestselling author Rachel Lee.*
Available June 2010,
only from Silhouette® Romantic Suspense.

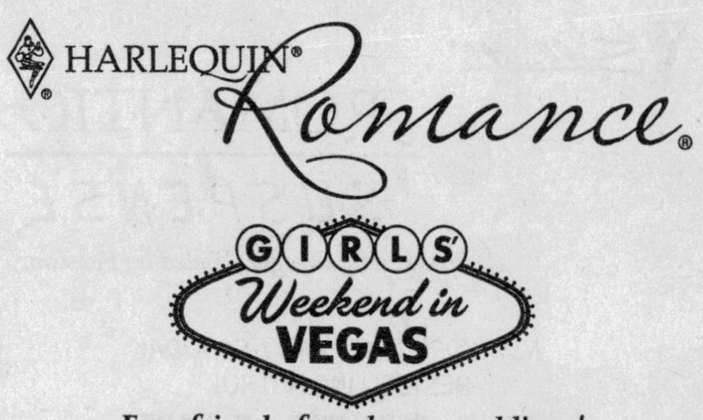

Four friends, four dream weddings!

On a girly weekend in Las Vegas, best friends Alex, Molly, Serena and Jayne are supposed to just have fun and forget men, but they end up meeting their perfect matches! Will the love they find in Vegas stay in Vegas?

Find out in this sassy, fun and wildly romantic miniseries all about love and friendship!

Saving Cinderella! by MYRNA MACKENZIE
Available June

Vegas Pregnancy Surprise by SHIRLEY JUMP
Available July

Inconveniently Wed! by JACKIE BRAUN
Available August

Wedding Date with the Best Man by MELISSA MCCLONE
Available September

www.eHarlequin.com

HR17663